D1795502

JUDGE ED

JUDGE ED

TED ROSE

Library of Congress Control Number: 2020903140
ISBN: Hardcover   978-1-7960-8784-0
                   Softcover   978-1-7960-8783-3
                   eBook   978-1-7960-8782-6

Print information available on the last page.

Rev. date: 02/17/2020

To order additional copies of this book, contact:
Xlibris
1-888-795-4274
www.Xlibris.com
Orders@Xlibris.com
809291

CONTENTS

PREFACE

WITH THE SATURATION of "Judge" shows on television these days, I began thinking that maybe I should be a judge.

Turn on the TV and watch as these 'arbiters of the law' hold what they describe as "court," and, then, become the star of the show.

We don't know what their qualifications or experiences are, or, even if they have a legitimate law degree, yet, they sit up there behind the bench and chastise, ridicule and, then, pass judgment on a lineup of wayward souls who stand there, on their best behavior, hoping for the judge to see it their way.

The judge badgers them and even tries to be funny sometimes while pretending to solve all their troubles. No jury... no prosecutor... no public defender... no witnesses... only their wisdom and insight as to how to settle the issues and save the day.

So, I decided... why not Judge Ed?

The same ground rules would apply to Judge Ed as they do for all the other judges, but, on a much more profound and grander scale.

Bear in mind that the descriptions of a few of Judge Ed's legal decisions and advice are done with tongue-in-cheek...a mixing of satire and parody of the entire genre of "Judge" shows.

And, as he has set the bar high and is proud of never wavering from the rule of law, he may sometimes seem very confident. He has learned the importance of maintaining a stern façade at the appropriate times, but, he also can exhibit compassion.

However, there is more to Judge Ed's life than just his duties in the courtroom. I hope to show him as a man with many interests...a humble person who knows how to enjoy life.

There is his trusted aide, Wilbur, whom Judge Ed has adopted as his ward.

Will their friendship grow and be able to survive the regimen and stress of their busy schedules and daily activities at the residential complex?

How will the attention and fame that was thrust upon him as a result of his presiding over a spectacular murder trial very early in his career affect his life?

Will he find true happiness with a woman who sneaks into his life and steals his heart?

And, can Judge Ed successfully confront and defeat an evil plot, designed by an escaped felon enraged with hate and motivated by revenge, that will threaten his life?

So, let's see what goes on in the world of Judge Ed as he faces each day with vigor and optimism.

Here, then, is...the saga of The Honorable Judge Ed.

ANOTHER DAY IN PARADISE

I T WAS ANOTHER beautiful day in South Florida. The gulf breeze was as exhilarating and refreshing as it always is, and, the Herons and Terns were gliding the warm air currents over the shallow water looking for their next meal, which was swimming, unaware of their impending doom, just below the surface.

Every day brings something new to behold and experience, and, the peace of mind and happiness I was enjoying here in South Florida only validated why I established my permanent residence and legal headquarters in this sunny paradise.

On this morning, as it is every early morning when court is in session, the traffic coming into the parking area was starting to build. The incoming cars, SUVs and vans are waved, by the traffic-control crew, to the available parking spots in an orderly and efficient manner. After the people exit their vehicles, they are directed, in single file, through a metal detector before they enter the path leading down to the garden. They will also see a large sign stating that no cameras or cell phones of any kind are permitted in the courthouse or the garden area, and, they should leave them in their vehicle or they will be confiscated.

Anybody can be randomly selected to be searched, at the discretion of the security staff, but, no one complains. They are more than willing to pay their money and tolerate all the inconveniences for a chance to see me, Judge Ed, in action.

And, if there are those foolish enough to push and shove or even attempt to ditch up in the front of the line, they are promptly tasered by security and carried off and tossed into the nearest ditch where they are left as munching material for the lizards and gators. (Not really... but, they are sent back to the end of the line)

The anticipation of getting into the courtroom sometimes proves to be too much to bear for some individuals who insist on standing too long in the blazing sun. The emergency squad is called occasionally because a person standing in line has become light-headed and sometimes pass out. They usually are helped over to an area behind the palm trees and stretched out on blankets in the shade where they can cool-off and be hydrated.

I told the EMTs not to waste their time by speeding over each time they are contacted. I suggested that they stay at their station in case a real emergency should arise. I have a nurse available on-site who can attend to the basic needs of these people as they lie there recuperating. If it turns out to be something more serious, then, we will call them.

Most visitors come with pre-bought tickets, which is the smartest thing to do, but, others take their chances on buying their ticket at the ticket booth, which is adjacent to the parking lot, when they arrive. Usually, if you can get a place to park, then, there should be a ticket available.

Just about all the television networks and some cable companies, along with Court TV, have tried to persuade me to allow cameras in my courtroom for live coverage of the proceedings. It would be the "greatest reality show ever," they said. The whole world would be able to witness true justice at work as it actually happens. The possibilities would be mind-boggling, and, I would become more popular than Oprah, they promised. And, a few national radio programs attempted to entice me to allow a live microphone to be placed on my bench during each session.

But, I told them all that I didn't want to do it because with "live" cameras and microphones in the courtroom the defendants would be prone to act like someone they are really not. They would no doubt engage in theatrics and be profiling for the cameras, and, therefore, detract from the integrity of the trial. And, it could even create a circus atmosphere which would not be a good idea. But, I also indicated I will leave the door open for such a venture if I decide to do it at a later time. After all, I can end it as quickly as I started it if things would begin to get out of control.

The sun was starting to warm things up on this beautiful morning and I had just finished swimming my daily laps in the pool. I poured some iced tea for myself and Mick Jagger, who was staying in the guest house for a couple days for some R&R. "Werewolves of

London" was playing on the stereo system, and, while I was drying off I noticed the time on the clock...it was later than I thought. Wilbur was suppose to have come over to alert me to the time about ten minutes ago, but, he failed to show.

It was now time for me to head up to my chambers to prepare for the day's docket. My robe should be hung-up (I hope) on the closet door ready for me to put on just before I enter the courtroom. My first case was at 10 AM and I was hoping that Wilbur had completed his chores instead of losing track of time working in the garden. I had a feeling that's where he was since he didn't show up down at the pool.

Mick said he would hang around the pool a little longer, if that was okay with me, before flying to Denver for their concert the next night.

He gave me a hug and then I headed up the walkway toward the back door of the courthouse to begin another day on the bench. The people who had made the trek to my courtroom deserved to see the best that the justice system has to offer, and, that's what I intended to give them.

THE COURT OF JUDGE ED

MY EXPERIENCES IN the courtroom have taught me that most of the offenders who appear in front of my bench tend to have a propensity for incriminating themselves when given the chance. I just allow them an opportunity to speak for a few minutes in their own behalf, and, usually, after bouts of incoherent mumblings and doubletalk, they remove all doubt as to their guilt.

Yet, as an optimist, I am always looking for some type of basic reasoning skills and maybe a glimmer of genuine remorse that might persuade me to consider leniency, and, be inclined to offer some hope for their future.

But, unfortunately, that doesn't happen very often.

And, as is the case for the majority of the trials in my courtroom, there is no jury, no prosecutor, no witnesses, no public defender and no cross-examination.

However, this format is waived for certain powerfully critical trials, the results of which will certainly have an impact on the public's opinion regarding the credibility of the justice system, and, are destined to capture the attention of the entire country. They are therefore perceived to be too important to be deprived of the usual trappings of standard courtroom procedure and protocol. The Roth murder trial is a perfect example of this.

I thought I would provide a sample of some of the requests and exchanges of communication that come from attorneys of people that have appeared in my courtroom over the years, and, their slick attempts to influence my decisions.

This case pops to mind:

In regard to the motion you recently submitted to the court, you are asking for a reduction in sentence for your client, Dawg Williams, due to, as you noted, his "experiencing such cruel and unusual treatment and punishment as he serves his sentence." This, you say, should not be an integral part of his period of servitude to Mr. Ashby as declared by "writ of mandamus" 16 months ago.

You cited a specific incident:

Whereas Mr. Ashby ordered your client to clean the leaves and dead bugs out of his swimming pool using a long-handled scoop that was stored in the tool shed. After making sure that Mr. Williams knew where the tool shed was, Mr. Ashby then went inside his house to his air-conditioned den to watch the football game on TV and enjoy a cold beverage.

After about 40 minutes, the scorching sun began to take it's toll on Mr. Williams. His legs were starting to cramp and he was becoming dizzy and disoriented. But, he remembered Mr. Ashby telling him, "Don't quit until the job is completely finished," so, he sucked it up and kept at it.

As he started scooping the surface of the water further out toward the middle, he reached out too far, lost his balance and did a belly-smacker in the deep end. Just then, Mr. Ashby was coming out to check on the progress of the work and saw Mr. Williams in the water thrashing and splashing around... like he was having a good time, when, in fact, he was just trying to survive above the water as his leg muscles started to severely cramp.

Mr. Ashby thought Mr. Williams had blown off the cleaning and was taking a swim instead. He did not like this at all, especially since he had just told him a few minutes earlier to keep working until the job was done. Not only did he ignore Mr. Williams' frantic plea for help (Mr. Ashby claimed he thought his shouting was all in fun...that he was just yelling at him to jump in the water with him), but, he also picked up a metal pool chair and hurled it in the pool in disgust as Mr. Williams was trying to dog-paddle, with only the use of his arms, over to the ladder on the side of the pool.

Unfortunately, the chair flew very close to Mr. Williams and one of the legs clipped his head and sliced his forehead causing him to bleed profusely into the water. After going under a couple of times, he finally managed to make it to the side and hang on until he caught his breath, and, then was able to pull himself out. He used a wet towel to apply pressure on the gash to stop the bleeding and then had to lie down in the shade on the deck of the pool for a few minutes in order to regain his senses and get his sporadic breathing under control.

According to my client, Mr. Ashby never once checked to see if he needed any assistance or even offered him water. As he was going back inside to get another beer, Mr. Ashby hollered back at my client to stop whining and just put a band-aid on the cut and everything will be fine.

And, by the way, because it was his blood in the water he had to drain the pool completely and refill it with clean water.

After reviewing the contentions and giving them careful consideration, I see no evidence which allows you "cause of action" due to any negligence on the part of Mr. Ashby. He reacted like any other normal person would under the circumstances.

Motion is denied.

SOME BACKGROUND

WAS SPRING-BOARDED TO the national scene as a result of the Dr. Benjamin Roth murder trial. It was an event that had captured the attention of the entire nation, as well as other countries, and, before it was over, it had evolved into a frenzied vortex of media coverage...something that had the potential to get way out of hand.

Satellite trucks, control centers, cable flat-beds and broadcast booths were all anchored on the street in front of the courthouse. Reporters and journalists from all sections of the country milled around the neighborhood looking for any news with which to fill the air time. They interviewed everybody from a elderly lady walking her cat to two sewer-repair men who had just crawled out of a manhole. They were all just hanging around waiting for the nod from me to begin setting up all their equipment inside the courtroom and have everything cranked up and ready for the big show.

They never considered the possibility that the go-ahead would never be issued. They had no idea they were in for a long and disappointing wait.

I did not expect to become an instant celebrity by just doing what the citizens expect me to do, which is to conscientiously fulfill my duties as a curator of the law. I never anticipated nor felt comfortable with the publicity I received as a consequence of the trial. I did manage to avoid any contact with the media during it's progress, but, after the trial was over, that was another story.

I was assigned the case, as I was told, because of my growing reputation as a fair and impartial judge who understands the law as well as about any judge. I had only been on the bench for less than three years, so, I was proud to be recognized for my work and honored to be offered this opportunity.

I am humbled by my good fortune to have inherited my ability to command the proceedings in a courtroom from my father. He was a natural at being 'in charge' of a class...not by stomping around the room shouting and wielding a yardstick but rather by displaying total confidence in his abilities as a professional. He was a high-school math teacher for 35 years, but, he really didn't have to teach all that time since he already had a decent income from property he had bought early in his career and was leasing to retail businesses. But, he stayed in the game because he loved the challenge and gratification of giving youngsters the opportunity to learn how to think.

He didn't talk about school much when he was home, but, sometimes at the dinner table he would open up and reveal insights on his philosophy of teaching. One of his principles that struck me hard during one of those conversations was that a big part of his success was due to his practice of expecting the same behavior from all students...not trying to patronize or compromise, but, establishing rules and then applying those rules to everyone. It's not a popularity contest, students can see right through you if you try to be somebody you're not, he would say.

He was also quick to point out that there can be mitigating circumstances involving students that might present an exception to the rule...like maybe a family problem or a personal crisis that might be best served by bending the rules a little bit and making a temporary adjustment to their academic regimen. Reward them for their determination to fight back from whatever it was that stalled their progress...give them some extra room to achieve.

Many of his former students, whom he would happen to see somewhere or receive a note in the mail, would tell him they now realize how much they appreciate his insistence when they were in his class that they utilize their talents and not be afraid of success. Seeing and hearing all this positive feedback my father received confirmed for me that he must have been doing it the right way.

I remember one time asking him what was the most important component of being a good teacher.

He answered, "Respect, son...once you earn their respect, then, the rest is as easy as falling off a log."

I feel very fortunate to have acquired some of those same ideals and principles, and, try to conduct myself on the bench as he did at his classroom desk.

From my experiences when I was a DA, and, as the OJ fiasco displayed, I learned that a shrewd trial lawyer can skillfully take the focus off of the prime suspect (his client) and divert it to someone else, thus, putting them 'on trial.' Then, he has the upper hand and the momentum in his favor. All you need is a judge who will acquiesce to this sort of strategy.

The defendant, Dr. Roth, and his team of attorneys, were glad to know that I would be presiding over the trial because they thought a young, lesser known judge with minimal experience would be easier to manipulate and intimidate. In their estimation, I was a judge who seemed like the perfect dupe to dazzle with their smooth rhetoric and persuasive powers, which were honed to a fine edge through years of trial experience that most always resulted in another verdict in the win column for them. Their case, they thought, would be better fought in a courtroom where the judge was just a mere formality... someone who would just 'Emcee' the proceedings and allow the attorneys to go down any irrelevant legal path they desired so as to accomplish their goal of distracting the jury from the preponderance of incriminating evidence against their client.

And, it would be icing on the cake when they would convince me, before the trial began, to allow cameras inside the courtroom... so the whole world could watch the drama unfold and see the great American justice system exonerate a falsely accused man.

However, as they would eventually find out, their grandiose plans to run roughshod through the trial would be stopped dead in it's tracks. They had no idea with whom they would be dealing and what awaited them in the court of Judge Ed.

THE MURDER

D R. ROTH WAS an acclaimed plastic surgeon and philanthropist... known internationally for his exceptional generosity and humanitarian efforts. A great man who donated his time and skill to repair and replace flesh that was torn or burned off the bodies of innocent civilians who were injured by collateral damage during civil wars in various African regions. He also traveled to other parts of the world which were in need of his expertise to treat victims of catastrophic natural disasters, industrial accidents or oil refinery explosions and fires. He could perform magic restoring faces and creating new ones.

He was the main innovator of the new and break-through procedure of facial transplants. Not only replacing the skin, but, also, the underlying bone, nerves, arteries and tissue available from organ donors. And, he was one of only a few surgeons who could keep the immune rejection rate under 10% by being able to determine the correct doses and selection of the anti-rejection medications.

But, as it is with all humans, Roth had a flaw. He could not stay true to his wife of 19 years and was having an affair with a woman who was 20 years younger than him. She worked as a RN in a hospital where he performed some of his surgery.

And, as it usually happens in these situations, their relationship hit a major bump in the road when one night, as they were cozy under the blankets, she let on that she needed more attention and maybe an allowance so she could buy some things to fix up her apartment a little. And, maybe some jewelry. And, maybe go out for a beer once in a while. She was starting to think, she told him, that maybe he was taking her for granted and really didn't love her like he said he did.

Her sudden revelation took Roth by surprise. This didn't sound like the girl he had come to know since the affair started about three months ago. She was always so agreeable and understanding.

She never complained and was always available whenever he called. He thought maybe he did get too complacent about her affections, but, she had to understand their delicate situation. They both were aware from the get-go of the circumstances. He could only come over maybe once a week and they couldn't go anywhere. And, he could only come over at night. I mean...come on, he thought...there were certain restraints here.

He tried to change the subject and sweet-talk her by commenting how sexy she looked in the candlelight and what a fantastic lover she was, but, she didn't want to hear it. He finally realized that he was wasting his time trying to assuage her tonight.

He had drank too much Maker's and was now starting to feel mentally and physically drained, so, he was not in the mood to deal with her sudden mood swing any longer. This was not the time to cross swords with her, so, he crawled out of bed and got dressed. He told her, as he was putting on his shoes, that he would think about what she said and the next time they were together they could discuss it further.

As he was opening the front door to leave, thinking that she would probably wake up the next morning and not even give their argument a second thought, she came out of the bedroom and yelled at him that he better think hard about what she just said because if he didn't agree to her demands, she would go to his wife and tell her everything.

When he closed the door behind him, the first thought that struck him was how surprised he was that she would go off on this crazy stuff...right out of the blue. He couldn't remember a damn thing he did or said that might have set her off.

And, secondly, he knew if he did start this game, there would be no end to it...the woman would want more and more money and still might bust him to his wife.

He decided to give her a chance to change her mind, so, he called her the next night. (Which was definitely a mistake, as were all his calls to her. Phone records are easily obtained by a judge's warrant and can be very implicating evidence if used properly by the prosecution.)

When she answered, he said, "Hi, honey, it's me, have you cooled down a little bit and thought about what you said last night? You really didn't mean it...did you?"

She shot back, "Yes, I did mean it and don't call me honey," and, then, hung-up.

He thought about driving over to her place the next night and trying to reason with her and get her to understand his position. But, that crazy idea lasted about five seconds...he must be going nuts to think that could be a possibility. She probably felt real good about finally having the nerve to confront him about all this and she obviously wasn't going to back down now.

He, the famous Dr. Roth, could not risk the possibility of being publicly disgraced, as well as enduring an ugly and costly divorce. He really wasn't too concerned about the humiliation his wife would suffer, or, the fallout that his two teen-age sons would experience... he cared only about his own reputation and the huge hit it would take. If the press ever got a hold of this one, his golden image would be tarnished beyond repair.

As he sat in his study watching the news on a stormy night, he decided this woman was not going to soak him or take him down. He never thought he had the capacity to even consider committing murder, but, then, he was never before in a situation this drastic. There were no second thoughts about what he needed to do. There really didn't seem to be any other viable alternative...he had to whack her.

After considering all the possible options, he decided to use cyanide powder to get her body to assume room temperature. It was a rather common poison and one that the CSI's could probably detect without much trouble, but, he figured he had that problem solved.

There was a certain protein, which was part of his arsenal of anti-rejection drugs, which would neutralize the poison's presence in the blood stream due to some cellular reaction. Thus, when they did the autopsy it would be very difficult to determine the cause of death...at least that's what he thought. If he would have taken the time to check out the properties of the protein before killing her, he would have found that the result he wanted out of this molecular combination was not possible.

He called her a week later and told her he would be over the next night and that he had a surprise for her.

When he pulled into his usual spot by her apartment door, he sat in his car for a few moments and took some deep breaths. This was it, there was no backing out now. It's just too bad she had to babble on about such ridiculous things, but, damn, she brought this all on herself. And, in congruence with his delusional and pathological dark side, he thought to himself, "What a waste...she was such a good RN."

He got out of his car and quickly scanned the lot for anyone parking their car or just leaving who might notice him go in her door. All clear.

As soon as he walked in the door she ran up to him, gave him a hug and whispered in his ear, "Hi, baby...what's my big surprise?"

He told her that he loved her very much and promised that eventually they would be together permanently...he just needed a little time to loosen up his wife before he asked her for a divorce. And, not only that, he would also give her some money that night.

She was ecstatic with the news and told him how much she loved him. As they embraced and kissed, he thought about strangling her right then and getting it over with real quick, but, no, he was not going to alter his plan.

While she was in the kitchen getting some cheese and crackers, he grabbed two wine glasses out of the cabinet. He opened the bottle of wine he brought, and, then, using his handkerchief so as to not leave prints on the opener, the bottle or her glass, he filled both glasses. The plan was that just before they clinked their glasses and took the first sip, he would ask her to please pour a little more in his glass for him...that way, her prints would be on the bottle. When the investigators dusted the bottle, it would certainly raise a red flag if there weren't any prints at all. He had to make it look like she was drinking the wine by herself.

He dumped the cyanide and the supposed neutralizing agent in her wine just before she came out of the kitchen and sat down next to him on the couch. She set the plate with the food on the coffee table. Then, she grabbed the bottle, at his request, and poured some more wine in his glass, set the bottle back down, and, then, they toasted each other for a long, healthy relationship.

Cyanide prevents the red blood cells from absorbing oxygen...a process known as "internal asphyxia." It only took a few minutes for the poison to take effect. She started to gasp and wheeze and then lurched forward and collapsed on the floor. He stood up and stepped back as the wine spilled out of her glass onto the couch and carpet when it fell out of her hand as she went down. As she lie on the floor sucking the air for oxygen, she started to turn blue, and, then, after a few more violent heaves, stopped breathing.

He picked his glass back up off the table and left everything else as it was, except he turned on the TV (using a handkerchief) so it would look like she was home for a quiet evening by herself. He also put some of the cheese and crackers in his pocket so as to make it look like there was only enough on the plate for just one person. He wiped his prints off of the doorknob on the way out.

It really didn't matter to him if they figured out the cause of death because no one knew he had been there anyway. He always kept his visits late at night and made sure no one saw him near the apartment. He thought, even if they did determine that she was poisoned, there was no way they could pin it on him.

SOMEBODY IS WATCHING

WHAT ROTH DID not know was that her ex-boyfriend, Carl, had been casing out her apartment periodically for about four weeks.

He had repeatedly tried to contact her and even left messages on her answering machine after their breakup four months ago asking her to give him another chance...he would do better next time and stop thinking only about himself. He even called after she started seeing Roth. But, she never answered because she didn't want to get in a talking match with him and take the chance he might think there was still hope for them getting back together. He might think she was leading him on and then start showing up at her apartment unannounced and that definitely couldn't happen. And, she was afraid to tell Roth about the calls because, with Carl being a nuisance now, he would probably think it was too big a risk to continue seeing her and cut her loose. She didn't want to jeopardize her relationship with Roth, so, she continued to ignore the calls.

Since she never answered or returned any of his calls, and, being the wacko jealous type, unable to bear the thought that maybe she was seeing another man, he decided to stake-out her apartment...it was time to find out what the hell was going on.

So, a couple nights a week, he would pull his van into a parking spot adjacent to her apartment, turn off the engine and wait. Most of the time while he sat there he listened to music on his Ipod while wearing head-phones...why wear the van's battery down, he thought. Plus, somebody might hear the van radio and come tap on his window and ask why he was just sitting in his van...doing nothing. They would probably wonder if he was a narc...a pervert?...a stalker? Some nosy neighbor would call 911 in a rash response of 'civic duty' and tell the operator there was a strange man, who might be a terrorist or something, hunkered down in a van in the parking lot...better send the police. In just a few minutes, the place would be swarming with cops and they would haul him down to the station for interrogation. Even though he was not doing anything illegal, he didn't want the hassle this potential scenario could cause....not a good idea.

For the first few weeks or so, nothing out of the ordinary happened...just her going out a few times to the store or whatever. He was getting to think that maybe this was a little ridiculous... slumped out of sight in the back seat of his van, trying to stay out of view of anyone who might walk by. Maybe he should just let it go and move on with his life.

Then, on a night when he was bouncing around the idea that this would be the last night he would waste his time acting like some pathetic vice-squad cop and just go on home and forget the whole thing, he suddenly saw a car pull in the lot and park right by her door. Now maybe something's going on after all, he's thinking...let's see what this guy is going to do.

He always kept his video camera in the van just in case something unusual did happen, so, he quickly grabbed it from behind the passenger seat and started to record.

The driver got out of the car, took a quick look around and then let himself in her apartment with a key. He leaned back in his seat with a smirk on his face and a chill in his heart. He put the camera on pause and waited for the man to come out.

About an hour later, the door opened and Roth came out, quickly got in his car and drove off, unaware that he had been taped.

Carl's initial reaction was that he should confront Roth the next time he showed up...just do a John Wayne and walk right up to him as he got out of his car and tell him what he thought about his late-night visits, and, then, stomp him. But, he nixed that idea because he thought the guy probably carried a gun and he wasn't ready to have a wild-west showdown with the man right in the middle of the parking lot just yet. It might look good in the movies, but, the hard reality was he had to be a little cautious and not allow his jealousy inflamed urge to pulverize the guy overcome common sense.

He wanted to try to get some sort of a physical profile of Roth from a distance before he made his move. How big was he?...how old did he look?...was there a pattern to his visits? And, he was curious to find out if they would ever leave her apartment together, which would probably indicate the guy wasn't married.

Maybe Roth wasn't the only suitor she had, he thought...someone else might show up one night. But, he figured the odds were against that because he knew it wasn't in her nature to be involved in more than one relationship at a time. He knew from first-hand experience that she has a tough time interacting with just one man, there is no way she has the capacity emotionally to deal with two or more men at once.

He even thought about following him in his van when he drove off, to find out where he lived, but, he didn't want to chance being spotted when he was trying to stay on his tail. Besides, his Jaguar would probably be a mile down the road before he could even get out of the parking lot. It would be like a mule trying to chase after a thoroughbred racehorse. So, he decided to just keep hanging tough with his surveillance for a while longer. Maybe something else might happen that could help him come up with a strategy.

During the next four weeks he took six more videos, three of Roth going in and three of him coming out, using the zoom close-up lens. He also zoomed in on the license plate each time he drove in.

On the night of the murder, Carl had no idea, as he sat in his van waiting for him to come out and wondering what the hell was going on inside, that Roth, at that very moment, was in the process of snuffing out his girlfriend's life.

Then, when Roth came out of the door and climbed in his car, Carl taped him and then turned off his camera. That was it, he thought, he had enough on tape now, it was time to make some decisions. He turned the ignition key, dropped it in drive and slowly pulled his van out of the parking lot and headed home. Before he had gone halfway, he finally made up his mind. He would blackmail Roth the next time he showed up. He would stop him before he could get in his girl's door and show him the video he had just finished recording of him leaving her apartment that night.

He was going to squeeze him for some dough. Why not?, he thought. He might as well get something out of this. If his feelings were going to be trampled on and discarded then he was going to at least make some money for all his suffering. After all, the turkey was obviously married since they never went anywhere together, so, he should be receptive to a deal. And, he drove a Jag, so, he had to have some big bucks.

The next day, while he was making macaroni-and-cheese for his supper, he decided to turn on the six o'clock news to see what the weather was going be that night. While he was walking from the stove to the kitchen table to sit down and eat, he froze in his tracks and dropped the plate of food on the floor as he stared at the TV screen in disbelief.

The lead story was about a woman that had been found dead by the police that afternoon. When he saw the reporter, who was doing the live report from the scene, standing in front of his girl's apartment building, he knew it was her...his instincts told him it had to be her.

A nurse at the hospital, who was a good friend, had gone to check on her when she didn't show up for work. When there was no response when she knocked on the door, and, seeing her car was still parked in her parking spot, she called the police. That was all the information the news reporter could give because the police had no further comment until the investigators had finished their work at the crime scene. And, the coroner would need a few days to determine the cause of death. (They had no trouble detecting the presence of cyanide in her blood)

He sat down on the floor and completely broke down. He was trembling with anger and fighting back tears knowing he would never be able to see her again to tell her how much he still loved her even though she kicked him to the curb. He decided there was only one thing for him to do.

The killer had to be the mystery man he had taped going in and out of her apartment all those nights, but, he also knew he probably would never be able to find him on his own so he could torture and then kill him himself. So, the next best thing would be to turn over the tapes to the police so they could find him.

How ironic that the video intended to be the means of a basic shake-down became, instead, the key piece of evidence that incriminated Roth and sealed his fate.

THE TRIAL

THE TRIAL WAS expected to last considerably longer than it did. The main reason it was swift and decisive was because I did not allow cameras or reporters in the courtroom as the defense attorneys requested. This was one angle that Roth had anticipated to utilize in his effort to sway public opinion and influence the jurors. They wanted the courtroom to be transformed into a 'stage,' like for the production of a television show, where the participants in the trial would become actors to be directed by the attorneys...as sort of a "reality show." But, at our pre-trial hearing, I blew that idea right out of the water. All members of the media were ordered to stay off of the courthouse grounds while court was in session.

I also warned the attorneys that if they had any plans for prolonging and contorting the proceedings with a display of legal antics, then, they would be severely reprimanded and threatened with possible dismissal as Roth's legal council. I had to chuckle to myself when I saw the look on the faces of the attorneys when I explained to them the expected parameters of behavior. They looked at each other like... what the hell is this...this judge wasn't suppose to say these things.

Roth was being charged with first degree murder. His entire defense was based on the theory that the girl's ex-boyfriend committed the murder. They said he had motive and could have gone into her apartment and killed her after Roth left.

But, even if he still had a key to her apartment it didn't matter because the apartment manager provided a maintenance report which showed that she had the lock on her door changed three months prior, which was soon after their breakup and about the time she started seeing Roth. His key could not have opened the door and there was no sign of forced entry. And, with the fact that she never answered his phone calls, she certainly would have never let him in.

All eight videos had the displayed date and time of the recording, which were authenticated by a camera expert who was called to testify by the prosecution. Not only was it verified that the time he was at her apartment was also determined to be the approximate time of death, but, the tape clearly showed him wiping the door knob with a handkerchief and carrying the wine glass in his hand when he came out of the door. His fingerprints were later found in other parts of her apartment that were left there from previous visits, which was a factor he failed to consider. The prints alone obviously did not portend he killed her, but, it did add another piece to the puzzle. And, the fact that there were eight videos of Roth going in and out of her apartment, and, the cause of death being poison, meant that the murder was pre-meditated.

After a last-gasp protest by Roth's attorneys that the tapes should not be admissible as evidence because of the possible violation of his civil rights by invasion of privacy, I overruled their objection and explained that I deemed them too critically relevant to the testimony of the ex-boyfriend to be thrown out.

And, of course, after I allowed the videos to be viewed in court, his conviction was going to be a slam-dunk. Roth and his attorneys realized it was over. They knew they had been beaten and that I, this "up-start, corrupt judge," as they portrayed me to the media, was responsible for swaying the jury to a guilty verdict. They made one more attempt at persuading me to consider some sort of a leniency for their client by asking for a plea deal, which I denied.

When Roth was brought in by the bailiff to appear before me on the day of his sentencing, he never took his eyes off of me the entire time he stood there. I got the sense that he was trying to detect a trace of pity on my face...some sort of a sign that might indicate I was going to go a little easy on him.

He never saw it.

I asked him if he had anything to say to the Court before I passed sentence.

He said, "Yes, your Honor, I do."

He then went on about his tremendous efforts saving human lives and his prestige in the medical community and so forth, concluding by saying, therefore, the "small impact of only one mistake compared to all the great things I have done should be taken into account and weigh heavily in your decision."

Actually, what he had said up to that point was basically correct… he did do all of those good things, but, his last statement went off the charts. I knew what he thought was sound reasoning was nothing more than a convoluted effort to rationalize the murder, even defining it as a "mistake." And, at the end of his discourse, he said, "Judge Ed, I throw myself on the mercy of The Court."

I responded by saying: "Dr. Roth, one life does not pale when compared to many lives. The fact that you have saved the lives of hundreds of people and mended many others does not, contrary to your opinion, diminish the sanctity of the life of someone else. And, when you chose to take her life for your own selfish interest by allowing your massive ego to prevent any rational thinking, you did not negate the importance or value of your past work, but, you relinquished forever the distinction, pride and morality you may have achieved."

"The Court therefore sentences you to life in prison…with eligibility for parole in 25 years."

I slammed my gavel.

"Case closed."

Once the verdict was made public outside the courthouse, the media were ignited into action, like a bear jolted awake from a nap by a gun blast. They ran with it for days and days, and, I was subsequently smothered with requests for magazine interviews, photo-ops, personal insight articles, talk show appearances and other such nonsense. They proclaimed it to be a great ending to a landmark trial. People calling in to radio shows and talking on the streets were praising me as a judge who made sure a man of such prominence and wealth got what he deserved. And, I didn't allow him to slither out of a conviction because he had me in his back pocket, or, because of some legal technicality miraculously discovered during the proceedings which would cause a mistrial.

The national consensus was that Judge Ed did it the right way and showed, by virtue of this trial, that justice can be swiftly achieved no matter who commits the crime.

HOME SWEET HOME

TO HELP FAMILIARIZE the reader with the surrounding environment in which I live and work, and, also, to set the stage for a terrifying sequence of events that morphed a routine day into a chilling nightmare, a brief description of my property and residential compound might be a good idea.

The complex consists of five buildings which are situated in the center of 350 acres of gulf-front property. There is a two-lane road off the main highway offering public access to the courthouse parking area only. This entrance is monitored by video cameras and is classified as "restricted" driving. There is the frequent presence of local police on patrol and a large iron gate that stretches across the road. It is opened only on days when court is in session. All cars are stopped and searched by a special unit of my security staff, and, only a pre-determined number of people are allowed to proceed to the parking area, the rest will be turned away.

There is another private road, which is also monitored, that runs from the highway to my compound. A large sign at the entrance warns drivers not to enter the road because if they do, their car's tires will be shredded by numerous spikes that protrude from under the asphalt over a stretch of about a half a mile. They can be lowered back under the surface by entering a special code number on my cell phone, on the terminal at the guard-house or the computer at my house. This road is used only by me, any maintenance or delivery people, guests and Wilbur.

One time, some idiot made a very bad decision and got behind the wheel of his '65 Mustang convertible after getting tossed out of a local pub. He was hacked-off because some honey had just played him off.

He had approached her while she was sitting at the bar with a girlfriend. He said that his favorite song was next up on the jukebox and he wanted her to dance with him. She told him she didn't want to dance with him when his favorite song came on the jukebox and told him to buzz off. Then, with absolutely no warning, he dropped his beer on the floor and reached out and wrapped his fingers around her throat. She screamed while her girlfriend started beating him on the head with her purse. The bouncers ran over and tackled him just as he was yelling he was going to rip out her larynx.

They picked him up, carried him out the door onto the 10-foot high deck and heaved him over the rail onto the gravel parking lot below. He laid there for a couple minutes, and, then, slowly got up and dusted himself off, making sure all parts of his body were still in working order. Then, determining he was far enough away from the bouncers so they couldn't get to him again, he threw a half-full bottle of beer he found sitting on the ground toward the door where they were standing. They ducked out of the way as the bottle flew over their heads and shattered on the wall next to the door. They yelled that he was dead meat and they were going to waste him right there in the lot. They started running down he steps, so, he jumped in his car and drove off, unaware he was headed in the opposite direction of where he lived.

After a few miles, he realized he was lost, so, he decided to take a shortcut by making a fatal wrong turn up my road. Whether he saw the sign or not, no one will know, but, it really didn't matter.

As he sped up the road, he either didn't know the spikes were there, or, if he did, he thought he could magically maneuver his car around and over them while going about 60 miles an hour. He managed to make it about 500 feet and then both front tires and one back tire disintegrated at the same time and the car was now rolling on the rims.

The car slowed as the wheels burrowed into the warm, malleable asphalt. Then, he lost control and banged into a ditch. He sailed up and out (not wearing a seatbelt) and landed head first in a clump of bushes. His body was mangled and blood was slowly seeping down his shoulder from a torn aorta that had popped through the skin where his neck had cracked open. He eventually would have bled to death as he lied there in agony, but, a Coral snake found him first and finished him off.

The action was all caught on tape, and, it happened so fast the perimeter guard had no chance to stop him. He notified the emergency squad immediately after the car went flying by the gatehouse, anticipating the disaster about to take place, and, then, coded into the terminal to have the spikes lowered for the ambulance.

When the squad arrived at the scene, they pulled the driver's body out of the underbrush and discovered that it was bloated to almost twice it's normal size due to the lethal combination of alcohol, 105 degree heat and the grotesque effects of the snake's venom.

While I was glancing through the detailed description and other information of the accident in a copy of the police report a few weeks later, I noticed a comment hand-written by one of the medics who attended the accident scene. He noted that he had been at the scene of many horrific accidents over the past 17 years of service and had seen lifeless bodies in all possible conditions, but, this one was extremely disturbing to him. He could not forget the hideous grin frozen on the dead man's bulging, red face when they found him crumpled in the bushes.

The entire perimeter of my land is surrounded by a 10-foot fence which is juiced with 2,000 volts of electricity. The radar system and other electronic surveillance equipment is located in a bunker about a half mile east of the compound.

And, if some deranged person breaks through the outer fence and decides to hike across my land to get a sneak-peak at Judge Ed or whatever, best of luck to them because patiently waiting for them to take the inevitable wrong step are quicksand, alligators, Coral snakes, wild boars, lizards and giant spiders that, with one bite, can completely paralyze a man in 30 seconds and cause such pain that he will puke up his guts just before he stops breathing. This can happen even before my security force can be deployed to confront the intruder and save him from an almost certain death.

Sometimes nature will exhibit her brutal forces, thus, temporarily relieving the field-security crew of their duties. They could be searching for a wayward trespasser, but, when they find him, all they can do is watch as he is chomped in half by a gator, or, just going under as he slowly sinks out of sight in a morass of quicksand.

THE BEACH

THE PART OF my land that I like best is the half-mile stretch of white-sand beach.

I enjoy the beach for many reasons. One is that it's the place where I have the best chance to become lucid, and, thus, give myself confidence I can make correct decisions. The serenity I feel allows me to focus with a clear mind on the issues that I face not only in the courtroom, but, also, in the routine of daily life.

It is undeniable that as we progress through life we are constantly confronted with a continuous series of decisions, some barely important at all, and, some very important, but, they all affect the direction and quality of our life. Success and happiness often depend upon giving yourself the best chance to make the right decisions. The beach is where I think I have the best opportunity to do that.

Landscapes always remain the same. Depending on where you live, maybe the leaves are off the trees for six months and on for six months, or, there might be snow on the ground for a while but that's about it...nothing else changes.

The ocean, however, is ever dynamic. It is constantly changing, sometimes very subtle and sometimes extremely dramatic, but, always transforming itself from one mood to another.

And, as I am in awe of the power and fury of the sea, there are times when it can also be very comforting and calming. Sometimes, when I am sitting in my chair on the sand gazing out over the water watching the waves lap at the shore and schools of sting-rays lazily gliding through the warm, shallow water, endlessly on the move searching for food, I will gradually approach a state of consciousness where I can reach total inner-peace

Nestled in the palm trees right off the beach is a small, two-story bungalow with a second-floor deck. On the deck is a wet-bar and hot-tub with a great view of the gulf...a nice place to hangout, with or without company, and, sip on a Margarita.

A fire pit is located on the beach at the bottom of the steps leading down from the deck. Sometimes it's nice to have a fire burning at night...it helps conjure up good memories and thoughts, and, it also keeps the sea monsters away. I like to cook just-caught crabs in a big pot of boiling sea-water hung over a fire on an iron spit, and, then, eat them right as they are pulled out of the pot. The meat is tastier when it is boiled in sea water instead of tap water.

The boathouse is located adjacent to the docks. It is accessible not only from off the water but also by a wooden walkway which leads to large double-doors on the east side. Here is where I can store my jet ski and a sailboat and fishing boat. All the fishing gear, snorkeling and skin-diving apparatus, beach chairs, umbrellas, skis and surf boards are kept on large shelves and racks in the rear storage area. Engine fuel is stored in a 200-gallon tank that is secured at the base of the north wall. It has an automatic pump-hose and nozzle that enables me to refuel the boat and jet skis while they are moored inside.

THE GROUNDS

THE FIVE BUILDINGS which comprise my residential complex are each constructed to my own specifications and design. Landscaping, architecture, furnishings, colors and amenities were all decided on by me. I enjoy doing some things myself instead of hiring someone else to do it. The adage: "If you want something done right... do it yourself," is certainly true. This was an opportunity for me to supervise the construction of my residence by creating from a vision I had fashioned over many years.

Security and the threat of hurricanes were taken into consideration as part of my master-plan. The construction of each building was done to accommodate a computerized security-system and to withstand up to 160 mile an hour winds. If there is any threat of danger, every window in each building can be automatically sealed in 10 seconds with a sheet of aluminum that slides out of the wall and locks across the outside of the glass.

The security is state-of-the-art, but, the fact is, a barking dog is really the best alarm system you can have.

I have three dogs, Curly, Larry and Moe, I rescued from the local humane society about four years ago. They are all mixed breeds with great personalities. They each live in their own deluxe dog house in a large area enclosed by a sturdy six-foot fence erected as a precaution against possible stray gators. But, they usually may go anywhere they want, including the beach, where they love to run.

I also have a cat, also retrieved from the animal shelter, that lives in the house. I thought I didn't like cats because when I was young my parents didn't want one so I figured I didn't either, but, I decided to give this one a try, and, to my surprise, I found out I like cats.

A three-hole golf course is located north of the compound. I usually send the dogs out first, before I tee off, to chase all the unwanted critters off the fairways and greens. I play much more relaxed knowing that I won't have to watch my every step and possibly find my ball crammed in the mouth of a large lizard or wrapped-up in the coils of a long snake daring me to grab it back.

The first hole is a par-three, the second is a par-four and the third is a par-seven. It was originally a par-five, but, I very seldom could shoot any lower than a seven on the hole, so, I changed it to a par-seven. Some of you avid golfers might be wondering how I can be so presumptuous as to change the par of a golf hole. Well, to paraphrase Willie Nelson: It's my golf course...I can make the hole any par I want. And, the good news is that my game must be getting better because now I'm shooting par more often.

An air-strip for private jets, located in the north sector, can be operational at any time. My secretary handles all transportation arrangements for my guests whether they drive, fly or cruise in to the dock on their yacht.

A large, above-ground, marine aquarium, or, what I call the "tank," is located half-way between the house and the beach. It is circular in shape and has a gradually sloped ramp leading up to a narrow, wooden deck that extends around the entire circumference. It is big enough to sustain eleven different types of tropical fish of all sizes and colors and also a White-Tip Reef shark and a Tiger shark. There is an underground observation room where I can watch all the underwater action directly underneath through the glass side and bottom. It's almost like I'm in the water with them, which prompts me to wonder if this is what it was like to have been Lloyd Bridges swimming around in the ocean in those episodes of "Sea Hunt."

For some reason, the sharks don't eat the other fish. I once asked the guy that comes to feed them why that was and I'm not sure exactly what he said. He was hard to understand and always seemed strangely distracted and nervous, like he was half-expecting one of the sharks to come flying out of the tank and take a chomp out of his head at any time.

The best I could get out of his explanation was something about certain chemical toxins secreted into the water from underneath the scales of the fish during times of extreme stress that repel the sharks.

If that's true, I said to him, then why doesn't somebody catch the fish, squeeze the toxins out of them into a bottle and sell it to swimmers on public beaches?

A questioned look came over his face, as if he actually thought I was serious, and, seemed to be thinking about the possibilities of what I said. But, he quickly turned away and walked over to his truck to get more food while muttering something about the orange fish. I shook my head and went back to the house.

A girl named Melissa, whom I had met through a common friend, came over to the house a few times for some swimming and partying...she was hot. But, she always brought her miniature poodle with her because she said she just couldn't be apart from her "baby doggie." I didn't like the dog...it was very neurotic and was always yapping and running around like it was on three hits of speed. I even had to keep my dogs penned-up while it was here because I knew from their barking and carrying-on that they didn't like this dog either. And, there were a few times when I wished I could have pulled out my Macho 45 hand gun and use "Fifi" for some target practice. But, I was willing to tolerate the mutt in order to keep all my options open with Melissa.

It wasn't long before we had a few drinks and were splashing around in the pool and she forget all about the dog. So, of course, the stupid thing wandered off and found it's way down the path to the tank. It must have wandered up the ramp to the deck and started sniffing around the edge of the water and got a bit too close...got careless and slipped and fell in the water. It was then promptly inhaled by one of the sharks before it barely got wet.

Melissa all of a sudden realized that her dog was missing, so, we spent at least an hour looking for it. I finally decided to let my dogs out and they would track it down in no time. When they caught it's scent and followed it down the path and up on the deck of the tank, I knew what had happened. That was the last time Melissa came over.

THE MONEY TRAIL

'M SURE BY now the question on everybody's mind is: How did I come up with the big bucks to pay for all of this stuff? How can I afford to build such a tremendous complex in which to live and work merely on a judge's salary?

I dabbled in the market in the mid-'90's as it surged and I hitched on to the ".com" bubble as it continued to expand. It was a strong growth period for the market, but, it also was the forerunner to a dramatic decline. I was aware, from talking with a couple friends who are financial consultants, that the "boon" wasn't going to last much longer...that it was doomed for a impending meltdown because there was very little substantial on-hand capital supporting the ".com" companies. So, I took the hint and cashed in my chips and got out just in time with full pockets.

I also took a little of the money and invested in two high-tech companies that showed they were capable of excelling in the burgeoning world communication market. Fortunately, the companies competed at a tremendous rate, and, through shrewd management, produced a great deal of capital on which to expand and build their future. I did some profit taking at the right times.

However, most of my money was made through real estate.

I turned an extremely good profit on some land I owned on the coast of South Carolina. I purchased the property, about 225 acres, four years after I had graduated from law school. It first came to my attention when I read about the land in the listing of property sales prospects while perusing The Wall Street Journal for potential stock investments.

The financing was made possible partially as a result of my appointment to a judge post on the 9th Circuit Court of Appeals from the position of county DA, and, more importantly, the ownership of a deed to 40 acres of prime real estate in Ohio that my father had left me, which I used as collateral for a large down-payment.

I secured an exceptional deal as a result of negotiating under the shroud of the prospect of ensuing environmental and ecological restraints on the land imposed by the EPA, which included part of the property being tabbed as a "wetland." All the land-developers were consequently scared away leaving the table wide open for me. The market value of the property was way under-priced compared to other coastal areas of similar characteristics, so, I jumped on it and took the chance that something good might happen later down the line. As it turned out, my hunch was right.

I did, however, get a little help.

A friend of mine, with whom I had gone to under-grad school, was then working for the EPA. We talked occasionally on the phone to stay in tune with each other's lives because we had developed a good friendship since we first met when we attended a few of the same classes our freshman year at George Washington University.

Throughout the four years of school, we played golf occasionally, went to concerts, drank lots of beer and shooters, and, even dated gorgeous identical twins.

We really enjoyed being with those girls. They liked to do just about anything and we always had a good time. A couple of times, thinking they could pull a fast-one on us, they switched identities and thought we never caught on. However, we did know what they were doing and we just went along with it to get some laughs. But, then one night, we let it slip that we had known about their ruse all the time and that put an end to that ride. But, what the heck, did they really think we wouldn't figure it?

One morning he called me and said he had some information in which I might be interested, but, he didn't want to talk about it on the phone. Nothing "cloak-and-dagger" or anything like that, just a precaution you learn to take when you live and work in the nation's capitol. Since we both were in D.C. at the time, I suggested that we meet that night at The Lizard Lounge, a bar near campus where we used to hang out to get away from the books. He said that was a good idea, so, we agreed to meet there at seven.

It had been a while since I had been there so I was looking forward to seeing the old place again. When we started going in there our freshman year, the bar's surrounding neighborhood was rundown with a medium-crime rate...probably not an area to wander around by yourself at night. We were always alert when we walked back to the dorm at closing time and fortunately never encountered any major problems.

After a few visits, we got to like the place. It had a great jukebox, real cold beer, and, we especially enjoyed the assortment of people who would wander in...people from the full spectrum of society who would stop in for a few drinks and mix it up a little bit. No hostility...no arrogance...just down-to-earth drinkers who could tell great stories and argue about anything. We would laugh all night.

Like the time a half-baked regular named Winchester Shorty was going on and on about his Harley and how he used to ride it like the wind and bust it 100 miles-per-hour down the pike and never got hauled in by the troopers. He said that he was the main topic on CB chatter of all the truckers all over the country for a long time and was known, as he put it, as "The two-wheel legend of the open road."

He claimed that the Hell's Angels tried to recruit him once back in his glory days. From what I can recall his story went something like this:

"Yeah...I had just finished using the head at a rest-stop somewhere in The Sierra-Nevada Mountains one day, and, as I was walkin' back to my hog I heard a loud commotion. I noticed a bunch of bikers hangin'-out and causing some sort of disturbance with some tourists who had just gotten off a bus that had pulled into the picnic area. I think it was a group of church people by what was written on the side of the bus...something like they were the 'Baptist Brigade.' They were unloading their lunch baskets and brown bags to take a lunch break."

"I could see some woman over by the picnic tables jumpin' around and goin' crazy, and, pointing her finger at one of the bikers. She was screaming at him something about givin' back the sandwich he grabbed off the table after she laid it down on a paper plate for her son to eat."

"The boy, who looked about nine or ten, was standing behind her yellin' at the top of his lungs that he wanted his sandwich...right now. The woman whirls around and hollers at this kid to shut the hell up...she can take care of this hooligan herself. The kid immediately shut it and just backed off. And, the rest of the tourists, who were all standing around watchin', started in yellin' at the biker, too...callin' him everything from a freakin' child molester to a scum-of-the-earth pervert. The dude just stood there and smiled back...like he was really enjoying all the attention and verbal abuse."

"Then, I saw him take a big bite out of the damn sandwich, chew it for a couple seconds and then spit it out on the freakin' ground. He handed the rest of the sandwich back to the woman and said he didn't like it so she could have it back. As he was turning to go back to his bike, she threw the damn thing right back in the dude's face and everybody cheered...even some of the other bikers who were standin' there watchin' hollered support for the woman. I just shook my head and mounted up to get the hell out of there."

"As I was putting the key in the ignition, a big dude with tattoos all over his arms and neck came walkin' over to where I was at. He said his name was BoBo. He told me he had spotted me as I was standing there watchin all this madness and wanted to know if I was the famous Winchester Shorty, and, I told him, yup...that's me."

"He said that he was the leader or captain or whatever the hell he was of this pack of Hell's Angels and he knew who I was 'cause he'd heard truckers and other folks talkin' about me at truck-stops and rest-areas all over this part of the country, and, he'd always wanted to meet me. He asked me if I wanted to join up with them and have some fun. I told him I wasn't interested and that I was already having fun."

When I heard that, I'm thinking to myself that he probably got the crap beat out of him about then.

He continued: "I don't think he took too kindly to what I said. I could tell he was a little pissed and he said something like; Why do you want to play me like that... I'm just trying to be friendly? I told him that I wasn't playin' him like anything, it's just that they didn't ride fast enough and didn't drink enough beer to suit me."

"The dude just stared at me...he didn't say anything. I reckon he didn't believe what he just heard."

"I told him it was nice meetin' him, fired up the hog, did a wheelie around a camper that was parked by the shelter house, and, then, goosed it down the on-ramp. I looked back as I was kickin' it up to about 80 and he was still standing there...starin' at me."

We laughed.

And, then, there was the night Winchester was bragging that he once drove his hog from Columbus, Ohio to Dayton in 35 minutes.

I lived in Ohio for a while and I knew that it takes at least an hour and 15 minutes to get to Dayton from Columbus, so, I chimed in, "You couldn't do it in 35 minutes because you had to go through Springfield."

He chugged the rest of his beer, looked over at me with a big smile to show me the five good teeth he still had left in the front of his mouth and blurted, "THROUGH Springfield?...Hell, I went OVER Springfield!"

The place erupted. I bought him a beer and apologized for doubting him.

I slowed my Explorer as I approached the block where The Lizard Lounge was located and pulled up to a parking meter across the street from the bar. When I got out and looked around, I was surprised to see things were completely changed. It looked like a decent neighborhood now, with the area being revitalized with upscale stores, restaurants and the ubiquitous coffee shops.

Even the bar had a new sign above the door. It was a giant lizard, outlined in green neon-lights, wearing a bow-tie and top-hat, with a cigarette in one hand and a martini glass in the other, and, a big grin on his face. It was awesome.

When I walked in the front door, I glanced around trying to see if my friend was there yet, but, coming in out of the bright sunshine made it difficult to immediately focus on anything. I stood there for a few moments to allow time for my pupils to dilate enough to be able to see better in the dim light and penetrate through the haze of smoke. I heard "Heartbreaker" playing on the jukebox and thought to myself...the music in here is still good. I didn't remember it being so crowded on a Tuesday night when we were coming in here years ago, but, as a singles bar, the Lizard certainly had improved...there were some nice looking ladies in here now.

After I was bumped into a few times as I was trying to position myself in the crowd to have a better vantage point, I finally spotted him in the corner already seated at a table. He saw me and waved me over.

I made my way through the crowd toward the table and I could see the waitress had just finished taking his order and was heading back to the bar.

When I sat down, he stuck out his hand with a big smile on his face and said, "Hey, buddy, it's good to see you again."

I shook his hand and replied, "It's good to see you, too."

He said that he had taken the liberty to order two Jacks... "like old times."

"You must have read my mind, I was thinking the same thing."

"Great minds think alike," he said with a grin.

Then, while I was scooting my chair a little closer to the wall to get out of the way of the traffic in the aisle, the waitress suddenly appeared and set our drinks on the table. She gave us a quick look-over and said with a wink, "If you fellas need anything else, my name is Betty...so...just holler and I'll be around. I can hear real good...see my ears?"

She leaned over so we could have a closer look and I could see that she had three Budweiser bottle caps, attached somehow to a string, hanging from each ear. She swung them back and forth a few times and then turned to go to the next table. She looked back over her shoulder and said, "Now...don't forget to give me a yell."

I said, "You can count on it, Betty."

She giggled as she walked away.

We laughed and then clinked our glasses in a toast to good times.

He then began to tell me, with a very sad face, that he was worried. It seems, as he explained in a solemn tone, that his brother, whom I had met one time, had completely lost his marbles and was running around his house about everyday, "cacklin' and flappin' his arms and struttin' around thinking he's a chicken."

I knew I was being set up, but, I went along with him anyway.

"Did you say he thinks he's a chicken?"

"Yes...I did. It's an absolute mind-boggling sight to watch him doin' the funky-chicken in the living room and actin' like he's livin in a hen-house."

I continued playing the straight man. "So...why doesn't his wife take him to a mental institution and have him committed?"

"She said that she doesn't want to," he said.

"Why not?"

"Because she said they need the eggs."

I busted out a laugh loud enough that people seated at nearby tables looked over to see what was so funny.

After I regained my composure and took a guzzle of my drink, he began to tell me what I had been waiting to hear ever since he called me that morning.

He had inadvertently intercepted an in-house memo on his computer the previous week about the specific land in which he knew I was interested. It referenced that the property was going to be taken off the "hands-off" list by the agency, but, not before it runs it's course through all the levels of red-tape, maybe four to six more months.

I told him how grateful I was for the heads-up and he said that's what friends were for. And, besides, he owed it to me because I had been such a big help to him when he went through some depression during his junior year. I didn't remember him being depressed about anything, he always seemed in good spirits and could tell a good joke. I told him I was glad I helped.

We caught up on all the events of our recent lives and had some good laughs, but, three drinks was now our "safe" limit, so, we decided it was time to head home. I covered the tab and tip with Betty, and, I also told her that the next time I came to The Lizard Lounge I expected to see Rolling Rock bottle caps hanging from her lobes. She giggled again, and, said "thanks a lot, I hope you guys come on back again some day...I like you guys...you're kinda cute."

I never really noticed until that moment that she was a very nice looking girl with a certain attractiveness that seemed a bit different than the rest of the waitresses. She seemed to have a touch of class...a sparkle in her eye.

My guess was that maybe she was a student at the university attempting to fit in with the ambience of the bar while trying to make some extra money to help pay her tuition. She probably would have been a fun girl to know...a good personality and a good sense of humor.

We toasted our glasses once more and then drained the last sip. I knocked over my chair as we got up to leave but everybody was cool and hardly anybody even looked over at me while I was picking it back up.

We walked toward the side door to avoid the crowd up front and when we got outside, he leaned over and said, "It was great to see you, Ed, I hope you stay healthy and happy."

I gave him a hug and said, "You, too," and, then, we each went our different way to our cars.

The next day, I initiated procedures on the financing, and, after about two weeks it finally was approved. I wanted to get the deal done as soon as possible before the information started to disseminate and create a great deal of interest in the property from various entities. Fortunately, he had called me as soon as he found out because, ironically, I had casually mentioned to him a few months earlier on the phone that, after a little research, I became very interested in that particular piece of land.

Then, about two years later, a Saudi conglomerate, after scouting the coastline from the Outer Banks down to Savannah, decided that my land was best suited for their intended purposes. The lay-out of the coastal and inland shoreline and how it tapered to the water with small inlets allowing easy access by boat to the inner-shores, was very appealing to them. They wanted to build a resort and spa complex with condos, swimming pools, tennis courts, a golf course...the whole enchilada, so, they made me an offer to purchase the property. I countered with a price a little more than I thought they would be willing to pay, and, then, they came back with a number that I really wanted. I accepted, and, the deal was done.

It was such a beautiful piece of land, but, I fell in love with South Florida after I spent a little time there the year before, so, it wasn't too hard to part with it. I knew then I wanted to build my own home in South Florida and this was the way I had planned to make it a reality.

With the profit I realized from the property in South Carolina, I bought some coastal land on the gulf and still had some bucks left over to build my house, and, eventually, augmented by the money made from my two ventures into the stock market, the other four buildings as well.

THE BUILDINGS

THE HOUSE

MY HOUSE IS a two-story, early French-Provincial, similar to a Victorian style, and, it has 4,700 square-feet of floor space, with three bedrooms and four baths.

A spiral staircase in the center of the house leads up about 35 feet to an observation tower. This is where I go to see out over my domain and get a visual check of the land. Sometimes, when the night sky is clear, I climb up to the tower and enjoy a vintage Cohiba Siglo V Cuban cigar while I peer through my high-powered telescope to observe the wonders of the solar system and try to fathom the concept of infinity that is the universe.

On the west side of the house, there is a large, screened lanai off the living room, accessible through two sets of double-doors, and, a second-floor balcony off the master bedroom. They both have great views of the gulf and the spectacular sunsets. The fireplace, built mostly with rocks that were excavated during the construction of the house, is on the north side in the den.

The pool is on the South side, and, is both indoor and outdoor. The outdoor pool has blue and green underwater lights and is rectangular in shape. It has a three-foot diving board at the deep end, and, a large deck area with lounge chairs and umbrellas. The indoor pool is about a fourth the size of the outdoor and has a hot tub in one corner. There is an underwater passageway connecting the two pools, which extends under a glass wall, so I can swim from one to the other. It can be sealed off when not in use.

There are double-doors on the east side off the dining room which open onto a gravel walkway that winds through a lush, exotic flower garden. There are Bougainvillas, Gazania Roses, Hibiscus Macros, Lantanas, Dracaenea Fragans and Orange Blossoms that make the garden explode with vivid colors and fill the air with sweet fragrances. At the end of the path, there is cascading water that flows down a rocky rivulet into a pond surrounded by palm trees. And, there is a flock of pink flamingos that fly in periodically to visit the garden to preen and get a drink of fresh water. They are very entertaining and magnificent birds to watch as they strut around posturing and looking for insects, crustaceans and small fish on which to snack.

Not directly related to the house, but, a unique component of the logistics of the compound, is an underground network of tunnels which connect three of the buildings; my house, the entertainment center and the guest house. They can be entered through a hidden panel in a wall in each building that opens to a stairway leading down to the passages. (Wilbur and I are the only ones who know where the secret doors are located.) All three tunnels meet in a large room, sort of like spokes meeting at the hub of a wheel. This area has electricity, ventilation, a simple communication system, food and plumbing. If necessary, I could live in the "tomb" for about 30 days. There is also an escape tunnel, which extends out about fifty yards from the compound, that has a camouflaged, ground-level hatch.

Due to the sandy soil, I had to have an extensive support system installed, by using wall and ceiling beams and cinder blocks, as a means to prevent cave-ins. Unlike the underground residences in Australia, for example, where people choose to live in caverns that were blasted and excavated out of solid rock by mining companies searching for veins of opal, my underground labyrinth had to be fortified.

Surprisingly, as I discovered when I visited those Aussie caves, they are nicer than you would think from just looking at their exterior from a distance away. You can't really notice that there is anything there that's out of the ordinary when looking at the side of a large hill other than a door-sized opening at ground level.

But, when you walk through that entrance, you have entered another world. These cavernous domiciles can be very comfortable as living quarters when all spruced up, and, more importantly, they stay cool in the blistering sun. They are located in the middle of the Outback desert, in the central portion of Australia, right outside the small mining town of Cooper Pedy. It is hundreds of miles from any civilization, with the oasis town of Alice Springs being the closest inhabited area. Because of the continuous, extreme heat in this part of the country, many people want to live underground because they know that the ground and rock provide the best insulation possible. But, if you have claustrophobia, then these subterranean homes are not the place for you.

Why would someone who has all the best security want to have underground tunnels. I don't need them for security purposes. They do offer the benefits of shelter from F-5 hurricanes, or, if my compound was being attacked by an army of crazed terrorists, but, those are not the main reasons I put them in.

Ever since I started watching scary movies when I was a young boy, I have always been fascinated with the scenes where secret panels in haunted mansions or in an eerie Egyptian tomb would slowly creak open after being activated by a chanted ancient curse or a turn of a picture frame. Then, Boris Karloff or some other creepy person would slink out. I was intrigued by the mystery they presented, and, I always wondered where they led. So, I guess it's just a crazy fantasy that prompted me to do it.

THE ENTERTAINMENT CENTER

THE ENTERTAINMENT CENTER is a great place to go for a change of pace. I don't spend a lot of time there...maybe on a rainy off-day or a slow Sunday. It's used mostly by my guests.

It has only one floor, and, in the front section, there is a small movie and satellite-TV theater with a 90-inch screen. I occasionally watch recently released flicks, usually action or scary, or, sports on TV. I also enjoy watching The Three Stooges and Laurel and Hardy. I have all their movies and laugh practically the whole time they're on the screen. Recliners, a wet-bar and a popcorn machine provide comfort and refreshments for me and my guests.

The remainder of the floor space contains an area with a pool table and ping-pong table, and, the spa with a steam-room, shower and weight-room, is in the back portion. Also, adjacent to the east side, there is an outdoor basketball court and tennis court.

I don't play tennis much at all but some of my guests like to play. However, the main reason I have it is so my pal Mansy can use it when he comes to visit. We went to high school together and we're still best buds. He was two-time state high school singles champion. He never lost a match or set his junior and senior year.

Speaking of Mansy, I remember a case brought before me during my first year on the bench in my new courthouse by some guy who had a plastic pen-holder in his shirt pocket and was wearing a bow-tie when he showed up in my courtroom.

He claimed that Mansy had intentionally violated his civil rights. He was pressing assault and battery charges and "malicious intent to harm." Since Mansy requested that the suit be heard in my court, I agreed to listen to the guy plead his case.

(And, if it seems that there might be a possible conflict of interest in this case, let me assure you, my impartiality as a judge allows me to rise above any petty influences and personal feelings that might preclude an objective and fair decision.)

He was standing in front of me, kind of slouched to one side, staring at the floor and mumbling when he started to talk, so, I quickly admonished him to speak up and look me in the eyes when he addressed the court.

He was startled by my abrupt warning and he began to act nervous and was constantly squeezing his fingers, one at a time, always starting with the thumb. He had beads of sweat running down his forehead as he kept glancing from one side of the courtroom to the other as if he were looking for somebody...anybody...to give him some encouragement.

But, he soon realized that he was on his own now and panic started to creep onto his face. The spectators just glared back at him, with no trace of pity in their eyes, as they were poised on the edge of their seats. They smelled blood because they knew I was going for the jugular real soon.

I told him, very calmly, he had one minute to tell me what happened. He gained some composure as he mopped his face with a polka-dot handkerchief he pulled from his pants pocket and spoke, this time, just loud and distinct enough so I could understand him.

The gist of it was that Mansy asked him at a street party if he knew who he was. When he answered "No," Mansy dropped him with one punch. He said he had just started wearing new braces the week before the party and his lips and mouth were cut badly by the force of the blow and blood gushed out all over his new flowered shirt and tan pants. He also claimed to have witnesses to the alleged incident to corroborate his story.

But, this is why I don't allow witnesses in my courtroom. Their minds had to be clouded so badly with the hallucinatory effects of alcohol and drugs they no doubt had surging through their veins at the time, that what they thought they saw wouldn't even be close to what actually happened. Plus, witnesses can be bought-off and paid to say just about anything you want them to say.

As he continued with his whining, he further added that he had made numerous attempts to settle out of court with Mansy's dad, "Big Edgar." But, when he eventually received no satisfaction of apology, admission of guilt or any financial compensation, he decided the only option left was to take it to court. Unfortunately for him, it turned out to be the court of The Honorable Judge Ed.

After he finally finished, I informed him that I was throwing the case out due to the implication of only circumstantial evidence and I strongly chastised him for wasting the court's precious time with such trivial and unsubstantiated allegations. Besides, as I explained to him, he should have known who Mansy was anyway...it was his own fault.

I fined him $250 and imposed $100 in court costs, and, sentenced him to two days in the slammer for "intrinsic fraud." But, I knew he would be nothing but fresh pork for some of the "friendlier" inmates, so, I suspended the jail time.

Before he shuffled out of the courtroom, I gave him some last words of advice: "Stay home with your mom and don't go to anymore street parties."

I apologized to Mansy for causing him the inconvenience of having to fly in to be in the courtroom, but, I wanted him to hear the accusations against him in person. I told him that since he was here, he might as well enjoy the facilities and was welcome to stay in the guest house for as long as he wanted.

He graciously accepted my offer.

THE GARAGE

MY CUSTOMIZED LIMO, a dinged-up Ford pickup, a cherry-red Escalade, two dirt-bikes, an ATV and two golf carts are housed in the spacious, one and a half story garage, built of cinder block walls and a slate roof. I let Wilbur park his car, a Honda Civic, in the garage whenever he wants to...it makes him feel important, in a way, and, he even thanks me for it. I like that about him. "Please," "Thank You" and "You're Welcome" are words seldom heard these days, so, it's always refreshing to hear him express his gratitude.

It is Wilbur's responsibility to make sure the three overhead doors and the side door are shut and secured while he's anywhere else and when he leaves at the end of the day. Since the garage is air-conditioned, and, for security reasons, it is a good idea to do this. All he has to do is punch in a three-digit code number on the terminal on the outside wall.

But, I've certainly learned by now that I'm only dreaming if I think that's going to be a sure thing all the time. Sometimes, he spends a little too much time doing one thing and then gets behind on his other tasks and forgets what he should have done earlier. He is becoming more reliable now...he's starting to learn how to budget his time better.

I had two infrared, electronic scanners installed in the garage, one at each end, that detect and analyze motion. If there is no one in the building or near vicinity, after 30 seconds, the scanners tell the main computer to close and lock any open doors. So, if Wilbur forgets to do it, it gets done anyway.

The gas pump is located directly next to the Southeast corner of the garage. It is in a shaded area and is well protected by steel pillars. I've made arrangements for a fuel truck to come in about every six weeks to refill the buried gasoline tank and the gas tank in the boathouse.

The car-wash area is behind the building where a power-spray water hose with a soap-adapter and sponges are ready for use. Wilbur washes all the vehicles for me. He would do it even if I didn't ask him... he likes it. I've watched him and he actually whistles while he washes.

One Saturday morning last Spring, I was in a hurry because I had an appointment in town and I didn't want to be late. And, since my chauffeur has the weekends off, I needed to get things moving myself.

I hustled around behind the garage to see if Wilbur was finished washing the SUV. He must have heard me coming because as soon as I turned the corner and was getting ready to tell him to shake-it-up a little, he blasted me real good in the face with the hose. He started giggling and jumping up and down like a kid at the circus. But, after a few seconds, I think he began to wonder if soaking me maybe wasn't such a good idea. He became quiet and was looking over at the trees, avoiding any eye contact.

I could see from his puzzled expression that he was trying to decide if I was really angry or not. It was all I could do to keep from cracking up. I slowly walked over to him and in a stern voice said, "Give the hose to me and go sit down on the bench over there (I pointed)...I'll finish washing the car and then deal with you later...I'm in a hurry."

He replied, hesitantly, "Yeah...sure, boss...sorry about that."

I don't know how I kept from laughing.

As soon as he handed me the hose, I turned it on full-throttle and then drenched him from head to toe. Then, I covered him with a layer of soap and stuck the nozzle down his shorts. I couldn't hold back any longer, I was totally losing it as I watched him hopping around whooping and hollering while water and soap were gushing out of his Speedos.

About a week later, Wilbur was helping me do some paper-work in my chambers, when out of the blue, he looks up and tells me how much fun he had that day at the car-wash when we sprayed each other with the water hose. He said he felt us "bond" a little bit, because afterwards, when he got back to his place, he had a good feeling in his heart.

I was stunned by his sudden sincerity and candor, and, I was at a loss for words for a moment. Sometimes Wilbur will catch me off-guard. I cleared my throat and then told him that I also had a good time, which made him smile...which made me smile. As we continued working, I couldn't stop thinking about what he had just said and how much it meant to me.

Most of the tools and other equipment are stored at the east end of the garage, where the work on the cars is done. A mechanic comes in regularly to do repairs and routine maintenance, and, to make sure all vehicles are always running smoothly. And, I have instructed him that Wilbur's car also will receive regular check-ups and needed repairs. I'm trying to save him some money that he would have to pay some auto shop in town, and, also, because he has enough stories to tell as to why he shows up late once in a while and I don't want him to think he can use the standard "my car broke down" line.

The mechanic is extremely competent because he is a genuine expert on car engines. He was the chief mechanic for a prominent NASCAR driver for about six years and was quite popular and successful during his time at the track. But, he made some bad decisions in his personal life off the track and consequently ran afoul of the law. A sticky mess he created that could be described as more malfeasance in nature than sinister. A situation where, as he claims, he was in the wrong place at the wrong time.

However, there were mitigating circumstances involving his brother-in-law that could have some influence on the disposition of the case. And, because of over-scheduling of trial dates in the courts of his residential jurisdiction, his case was transferred to my court, with my approval. As I initially glanced through the case documents and records, I realized that due to the nature of the crime, he definitely had a good chance of seeing some time in the cooler.

When he was notified that I was going to hear his case, he soon submitted a request for a plea-deal. It is not unusual that defendants eagerly seek to negotiate some sort of 'modified' sentence before their trial date because they are aware of my reputation as a judge that is prone to apply the law to it's fullest extent. Most of the time, I refuse to even consider any effort to reach a compromise, but, I liked this guy for some reason, so, I decided to listen to his supplication.

He was a big, raw-boned man with huge, powerful hands, as I painfully found out as we shook hands when he arrived for his scheduled meeting with me in my chambers. They were rough and gnarled...like I would expect for someone who has worked in the oil-pits most of his life. His grip was like a steel vise and it felt like the bones in my fingers had just been crushed into little pieces like they were nothing more than stale pretzels sticks. I don't think he knew how hard he had squeezed my hand...I'm sure he was just trying to make a good impression and was a little too eager.

I didn't want him to know about the serious hurt he had just put on my hand, so, I gritted my teeth and told him to please sit down in the leather chair across from my desk.

I offered him some iced-tea. He said thanks, he would like some, so, I filled-up a glass (with my left hand) from the pitcher I was keeping in the mini-fridge and handed it to him. He nodded and then gulped down about half the glass and put it on the side-table by the chair. I walked over to the window and slowly closed the drapes to buy some time for the pain, that was now shooting up my arm, to subside.

After straightening a picture on the wall and getting some folders out of the filing cabinet (with my left hand again), I plopped down behind my desk. I sat there for a moment, staring at the computer, as I was trying to determine if I was now able to use my hand again. The throbbing had almost gone away, so, I opened the folder and took out all the documents, reports and testimonies related to his case and then looked up at him.

He had not uttered a word, other than "Thank you," the entire time I was moving around the room, even when I was trying to make casual chatter. I could tell he was nervous because he couldn't sit still and kept looking at his watch every fifteen seconds like he was expecting a car race to start somewhere.

I told him to relax and take another drink of his iced-tea, which he did, and, then, I asked him what his proposal was and what he wanted to offer me as his end of the bargain. I was a bit surprised when he replied, "Your Honor, I initially had a couple ideas to bounce around, but, the more I thought about it the more I decided they probably wouldn't work. So, I completely trust in your compassion.

I have nothing to offer that would be as fair and just as your decision will be...it's your call."

Why did he come all the way out here and then not follow through on his plea? I wasn't sure if he just didn't have the stones to actually suggest a plea, or, if he was being coy and hoping to win me over with his feigned praise. Whichever it was, he was right, it was my call, so, I offered him my solution.

I told him the best approach would be to "bifurcate" the case, which means to separate the issues to help facilitate their resolution. Specifically, go ahead and pay the brother-in-law what he owed to keep him quiet and make him disappear because, with his past record, he had the potential to be a definite problem later. Then, if this matter was handled judiciously, I would suspend his jail sentence if he agreed to become my "chief mechanic" for the equivalent amount of time.

And, at the conclusion of that period of time, I would then give him the option to continue working as my mechanic if I was satisfied with his work. The difference being, he would be on my payroll and start earning some decent money on which to live, and, also, it would help offset his financial losses due to the payoff and the loss of his job at the track. (He lost his gig at the track because of his legal troubles and probably didn't have much chance of hooking up with another race team in the near future)

The decision was an easy one for him to make and we both knew it. It was a perfect fit...he keeps my vehicles running and I keep him out of jail.

THE GUEST HOUSE

T HE GUEST HOUSE is a modest ranch style with three bedrooms and two baths. It is very cozy with a fireplace and a small lanai. (The guests may use my hot-tub and pool anytime) The exterior is 'Ocean Blue' in color with yellow shutters and flower-boxes under the windows.

The people who have stayed here come from all walks of life and have diverse backgrounds. But, the common thread that seems to run through all of them is that they are very successful in their chosen profession and have utilized their special talents to the fullest.

I like my solitude, but, I enjoy getting to meet and know all my guests. They were all very appreciative, gracious and extremely generous...much more than they ever needed to be. I always try to make it clear that they need not do anything for me because it was my privilege to give them an opportunity for some R&R. Everybody who has been here is so good at what they do that it was gratitude enough for me to see them show up spread kind of thin and dragging a little, and, then, leave with fresh ideas, fresh bodies and their motor running at top speed again. Whatever the reason for their visit, nobody leaves disappointed.

Some of the people who have been a guest include:

Bette Midler

She is exactly the same vivacious woman in person as she is on the screen. She is always in a happy-go-lucky mood and wants to have a good time whatever she is doing, the sort of person I very much enjoy... uplifting and outrageously funny.

Hunter Thompson

A gifted writer who was a prominent contributor to the literary assault on "The Establishment" back in the late 60's and early 70's. He created a kind of mad, caustic prose that told, from his political vantage point, what was really happening in the country at that time. And, he used hard-core humor to get his point across. He could be very funny.

Truman Capote

Another great writer. A very nice man, but, I learned not to be fooled by his gentle demeanor. He had a rapier wit and was always ready for an intellectual 'tete-a-tete'. And, I was well aware that I was way over-matched during most of our conversations even though I tried to hold my own. I usually did most of the listening. I loved to listen to him talk...very engrossing.

One time, when we were enjoying a glass of Caymus Cabernet Sauvignon in the flower garden, he told me how he writes his novels. He said that he always writes the last chapter first. I thought, that seems odd...how would he know what to write at the end of the story if he didn't yet know what he was going to write at the beginning?

A little later, after I popped open a second bottle and we were strolling among the beautiful flamingos that had flown in for a visit and were strutting around in circles by the pond, I think I finally understood what he was saying.

You hatch an idea about an event or a situation, or, a final twist that you think would be interesting and worthy of your effort, then, build your story to that point. You just can't start to write a story without knowing where you're going with it. You must have a vision as to how to get to the ending you want, but, you have to know what that ending is first.

It certainly worked for him.

Cal Ripken, Jr.

He is a class act all the way. A very proud yet humble man. One of the greatest players ever... epitomizing the qualities of dedication, determination and true sportsmanship on the field. His Major League record of consecutive games played is testimony to that.

During Cal's visit, Wilbur kept asking me, "Do you think he would play catch with me if I ask him?"

I said, "There's only one way to find out."

So, the next morning while Cal and I were playing with the dogs in front of the house, I noticed Wilbur kind of hanging around over by the garage...acting like he was busy doing something. But, I could tell he was just biding his time while he was working up the nerve to confront Cal. I considered waving him over but then I thought that maybe he needed to work this out for himself, so, I just continued bouncing a rubber ball off a palm tree for the dogs to chase and acted like I didn't notice him.

After about ten minutes had passed, he must have decided that the time was now, so, he started to slowly walk over to where Cal and I were standing. When Cal saw him walking his way, and, before Wilbur could say anything, he says, "Hey, Wilbur...how 'bout you and me goin' down to the beach and play some catch?"

Wilbur's jaw dropped to the ground. He was stunned. (I told Cal later when Wilbur was gone that what he did for Wilbur was awesome. He just smiled)

Then, after he was frozen in disbelief for a few seconds, he turned and started to run full-speed to his car while at the same time trying to jam his hand down into the pocket of his cut-off jeans to get the keys out. He finally got them out of his pocket when he got to his car but started fumbling and dropping them as he tried frantically to open the trunk. It was all we could do to keep from laughing out loud at the sight of Wilbur's excitement. He finally calmed down enough to get the right key into the lock and then opened the lid. He reached back behind the spare tire and grabbed his ball glove. Then, he turned and faced us, held it up above his head and hollered, "I'm ready!"

Cal hustled to the guest house and went in to get his glove. He came out the door a minute later and held his glove up and yelled, "I'm ready, too."

They started to walk down the path to the beach, so, I tagged along to watch the action. I used to watch Cal play on TV and there was no way I was going to pass up the chance to see him toss the rock around in person.

When we got down to the beach, I sat down on a dune and thought how lucky I was.

When they started to play catch, about 50 feet apart, I noticed that Wilbur had a darn good arm. He was really putting some smoke on the ball and so I yelled at him, "You got a good heater, kid."

He smiled. It seemed as though he had some natural ability and Cal even said he was impressed with the strength of his arm. Wilbur was really getting pumped-up hearing all the compliments, and, of course, his next throw went about ten feet over Cal's head.

Wilbur said he used to play catch with his dad when he was a young boy and tossing the ball with Cal brought back some sweet memories of that time in his life.

Wilbur was having a hard time catching the ball because his glove was in such bad shape with the leather binding coming apart and two of the fingers being torn. He never used that as an excuse, though, as the reason why he was dropping the ball so often. But, Cal saw the problem after a few tosses when he noticed how raggedy Wilbur's glove was. So, after they finished, Cal walked over to Wilbur and handed him his glove, a practically brand new one that he had used sparingly the latter part of his final season, and said, "Here, Wilbur, take my glove, I've got lots of 'em...you need this more than I do. When we get back to the house, I'll autograph it for you."

I'll never forget the look on Wilbur's face...he was flabbergasted (so was I) by Cal's wonderful gesture. The glove became such a treasure to Wilbur that there were times when I would see him working in the garden or cleaning the courtroom and it would be hanging at his side...hooked on to his belt. I guess he didn't want to take a chance that it would get stolen or lost, and, he was always ready in case I had some spare time to play catch with him.

Hulk Hogan

Hulk stayed for about five days, and, he asked if it would be okay with me if he invited a few of his wrestling buddies to come join him the last couple days so they could have a "last-one-standing" wrestling tournament down on the beach. It would be sort of a rehearsal for their upcoming annual "WrestleMania" event which would take place in three weeks at Madison Square Garden. I thought it was a great idea so I told him to go ahead and do it.

The thought of being a professional wrestler has always intrigued me. I know it's not real wrestling and the outcomes of the matches are predetermined, but, I don't care, and, neither does anybody else. It's simply entertainment, just like everything else that's scripted on TV. I think it would be a blast to assume the persona of some nasty, despicable character during the matches and put on a zany act for the purpose of making fans either love me or hate me, and, more importantly, keep coming back for more.

Wilbur came down to the beach after he finished his chores (at least that's what he said) and started watching Hulk and the boys perform all the flips, flying hammer-locks, pile-drivers, double arm-bars and kicks in the face. He was really getting into it...yelling and pointing his finger at Hulk...telling him he was all washed-up. It was hilarious.

He continued with his taunting and then began woofing at "Nature Boy" Ric Flair and telling him his mother wears combat boots.

Finally, Hulk said, "That's enough, pal," and grabbed him around the waist, lifted him up and started tossing him around like a sack of flour. Then, he gave him about ten airplane-spins and body-slammed him...sand was flying everywhere. And, after all that, he heaved him about 20 feet out into the surf with a big splash.

When Wilbur finally emerged from under the water and waded back to shore, he was smiling from ear to ear. Then, he shouted loud enough for all to hear over the roar of the crashing waves, "Well, I guess this means I'm not going to win the tournament this year." Everyone broke-up laughing and they invited Wilbur to join them for a beer for being such a good sport.

Tom Petty and The Heartbreakers

About a year ago, Tom Petty and The Heartbreakers stayed in the guest house for a few days. He wanted to take a break from his three month United States tour, so, he called my secretary and she patched him through to my cell phone.

He was real nice and complimented me on my service to the judicial system as a respected judge, etc.. Then, he got to the real reason for his call.

He wanted to know if he could "hang-out for a while at your awesome crib," as he put it. He had read about and seen pictures of my complex in People Magazine and decided that it looked like the perfect place for him to crash and burn for a few days. He was very apologetic and said he hated to ask this imposition of me due to the fact that he didn't know me and we had never met. I could tell from the tone and slight strain in his voice that he was in need of a self-imposed disappearance from the public and a brief hiatus from the rigors of the road.

After seeing him play at a concert a couple of years earlier in Miami at the Orange Bowl, I became an avid fan of his. Listening to music on the radio or a CD is one thing, but, when you hear the band in person, it's an entirely different ball game...it tends to stick with you a lot longer. He seemed like a genuinely nice guy on the phone, so, I told him there would be no worries and that he and the 'Breakers' could stay for as long as they wanted.

He said they would fly in the next Tuesday after his show in Atlanta. He also wanted to know if it was okay to bring a few ladies along with him. I said no problem. I would have agreed even if he had not told me that one of the girls he was bringing had seen me on the news one time and thought I was "kinda cute," and, she was looking forward to meeting me.

He wasn't very convincing, but, I knew he was telling me this as his way of showing his appreciation for my promised hospitality and I thought it was an amusing gesture. I just said something like, "Ah, shucks...you really don't mean it," and let it go at that. Why worry whether some babe has the hots for you or not...just have fun. I'm sure Tom got the message across to the girl about being nice to me while they were here.

I'll never forget his concert in Miami. I was asked to speak at a seminar at The University of Miami Law School on "The Triumphs and Failures of America's Criminal Justice System," and, by chance, his show was the next night. I usually don't like to call in a marker, but, I thought, this time...why not? I knew I liked his music and I thought this would be a golden opportunity for me to check him out in person. So, I made a call to an acquaintance living in the area, whom I had helped battle through an ugly divorce case with minimal financial damage, to see if he could scare up a couple of tickets.

He was excited to hear from me and said he would make a few calls and then get back to me. I had a feeling he could make it happen...he was a grateful man. Ten minutes later, he called back with two 10th row seats...right in the center.

The concert was really starting to heat up... everyone was singing along at the right times and Petty was really sounding great. Then, after about the sixth song, some awesome looking babe, wearing nothing but shorts and a tank-top, somehow eluded the front-line security, and, before they could grab her she climbed up on the stage and started dancing right in front of Petty. As the security goons came out from backstage and started to slowly converge on her, he waved them off. They turned and went back behind the back-drop, much to the delight of about 20,000 people who roared their approval. Petty was cool and never stopped singing. He made her surprise appearance blend right in with the song as she continued to dance and gyrate all over the stage. It was a masterful job of milking the situation for all it was worth.

When the song was over, Petty motioned to her it was time to leave the stage. She walked over to him and gave him a kiss on the cheek, then, waved to the audience and started to walk toward the exit in the back curtain where the security crew were waiting.

The crowd went absolutely berserk. We started chanting, "one more time...one more time," over and over. So, right on cue, he waved her back and said, "Let's do it again." The audience had completely lost it by now and we were in some sort of a raw trance while Petty and Miss X were stepping it out in the middle of the stage while the band was pounding out "Runnin' Down a Dream." Right then I became convinced that what I was experiencing, along with everyone else in that stadium, was, indeed, rock-and-roll nirvana. It was unbelievable.

The next morning, I was glancing through The Miami Herald while sitting out on the balcony of my ocean-view hotel suite and sipping on a Bloody-Mary. My body was still wired with left-over vibes from the night before at the Orange Bowl that had permeated my bones from all directions. Most of them had lost their charge but I still had some slight buzzing periodically, as it felt like a few were still bouncing around inside me like a pin-ball on the loose. I have been to many great concerts but this was one of the best. The residual effects that I was experiencing were a pleasant reminder of the intensity and almost electric aura that emanated from not only the stage but also as it engulfed the entire Orange Bowl. The Bloody-Mary seemed to help mellow-out the lingering tremors.

I thumbed through the pages of the paper looking for the entertainment section so I could read the write-up on the concert. In my opinion, the show was so good, it should have made the headlines on the front page, but, there it was in the music section, and, on the second page. I couldn't believe it. I wondered, was the person who wrote this article actually not at the concert to not be able to persuade the editor to put it at least on the first page of the section?

Anyway, the piece was very complimentary, with a picture of Petty and the girl dancing up-close on stage, with the caption: "Tom gets it on with mystery intruder." There was also a great deal of deserved praise heaped on The Heartbreakers and specifically, Michael Campbell, the lead guitarist.

I sat up a little in my chair as I began to read the paragraph about a reporter from the local TV station who yelled at Petty just before he jumped in his limo after the show and asked him if he was going to "bring trespassing and threat of physical harm charges" against the girl. How any normal person could ask an inane question like that after watching them dance together on the stage just a few minutes ago was incomprehensible to me.

He responded by laughing first and then saying, "The only physical harm inflicted by her tonight on me might occur in my plane in a short while after we take-off." I'm sure everyone chuckled at that one.

He continued, "but, seriously, she seems to be a dynamite lady and I've decided to keep her around and let her accompany me for the remainder of the tour...with her consent, of course. She may even do some more dancing."

When I read that statement, I knew it's intent was to sell a few more tickets for the rest of their current tour. (although, his concerts are usually sold-out anyway) He knew this girl was a gift from heaven and he wanted to see what would happen if he let her tag along.

I remember after I talked with Petty on the phone when he called to inquire about staying in the guest house, it dawned on me that she couldn't be one of the ladies coming with him.

I knew this because about six months after the concert I was scanning through an entertainment magazine while I was waiting in the dentist's office. I was getting ready to put it back on the table because the nurse had just walked into the waiting room to tell me that the doctor was ready to see me.

But, as I was closing the page, an article caught the corner of my eye. It was about Tom Petty and some recent events in his life. And, because of how much I liked his music and the memory of his great concert, the article piqued my interest. So, I hurriedly read the first few paragraphs as the nurse was calling me for the second and third time.

The article explained that the girl who jumped on stage with Petty that night booked-up on him and went back to her husband. When the reporter asked her why she left the tour and went home, she said, "I got fed-up with that sort of life...it was getting awful stale and the lack of sleep was making me act crazy. I couldn't live like that anymore and I realized I need to get some work done at my house. The kitchen needs to be re-done and I think I'm going to paint the walls a light orange shade. And, there probably is a lot of laundry to do."

When the husband was asked why he was letting her come back home after she basically turned into a drug and sex-crazed 'roadie' for about four months, he said, "What she did was like lighting a fire under our cold and paralyzed love life, and, I think it was just what we needed to re-kindle our romance and stabilize our marriage."

For some reason, I was not able to fully comprehend the two statements. They did not immediately compute. Maybe, it was because I read them too fast and didn't have time to absorb anything from the words that might make any sense. After all, I was being rushed by the nurse, who was getting a little irritated by this time. Maybe the moderate anxiety I was feeling about what I knew was about to happen in the dentist's chair precluded any possible logical interpretation.

I quickly put the magazine down and apologized to the nurse for ignoring her and making her wait. I explained to her, as I followed her into the room, that I really didn't mean to be rude, but, I had to read that paragraph about Tom Petty cause I saw him in concert about 6 months ago and was blown away.

She smiled and said, "I love his music, too. "You Wreck Me, Baby" is awesome." She was very nice about it.

As I sat in the chair trying to concentrate on something other than the whirring drill that was jammed in my mouth, I was still puzzled about what I had just read out in the waiting room. I couldn't help but think about those two people and wondered how many couples there are out there in the world that would feel the same way if they were in a similar situation.

But, maybe the woman did have it right. Maybe going off on some wild and schizophrenic ride through another dimension might be the thing to do to save a dying relationship and interject some juice back into your life. It could be that sometimes a temporary departure from one's norms and intrinsic values in a dramatic fashion can be a viable method of staying in touch with reality.

THE COURTHOUSE

THE COURTHOUSE IS a square, two-story structure that from the outside looks like a typical, small-town courthouse. It has four pillars at the top of five steps, with two on either side of the main door.

I had it built about 200 yards from the compound because I wanted it off by itself...to help deter trespassing, minimize security problems and to keep the occasional noise of the traffic and crowds away from the other four buildings. Even though it is on my property, it is a separate entity from the residential complex.

There is a rectangular, grassy area in front of the entrance with a fountain in the center that has a marble statue of a Greek goddess, with water shooting out of her mouth, wearing a blind-fold and holding the 'Scales of Justice.' The blind-fold, of course, symbolizing that justice must be "blind" in order to be true to the concept of pure objectivity.

The grass area is bordered by sea-lavender and camellia shrubs, with palm trees behind them. And, the alameda leading down from the parking area splits and goes around both sides of the garden and then converges into a wide approach walkway at the other end that leads to the steps of the entrance. On both sides of the walkway are beautiful orange blossoms, which is the state flower.

I do not allow the visitors to walk on the grass, but, they have the opportunity, if they so desire, to throw coins into the fountain while they stand on a small observation deck located next to the fountain.

The 'ritual' of throwing coins at the fountain was starting to become a nuisance. I was starting to question why I decided to allow what eventually evolved into a crude form of a carnival midway-game to take place right there in the shadow of the courthouse. Half of the coins ended up on the grass or even landing in some of the bushes that border the fountain. So, I had Wilbur draw-up a sign and post it by the deck that read: "Please, do not toss coins into the fountain...my bank is running out of space to store them. Thank You."

But, they keep on doing it anyway. Maybe they are wishing for good luck as they hurl their money into the water. Or, maybe they are showing their gratitude that they are not one of the unfortunate souls that must face The Honorable Judge Ed that day in the gray edifice looming in the near distance.

Whatever the reason, I decided...okay...if that's the way it is, then I'll use the money collected by Wilbur every few days from the fountain and the surrounding area to help pay for the transportation costs for groups of high-school students wanting to attend a court session on a field-trip or for a class assignment. It has turned out to be very popular because there is always a waiting list of schools requesting attendance instructions. And, my secretary does a great job of organizing all the scheduling and keeping everyone notified if there are any changes of times or dates.

The entire area is immaculately maintained by Wilbur. I commend him on his efforts almost daily. He takes pride in keeping this area beautiful because he understands that people feel good and are at ease when they are in serene and structured surroundings, and, can sense order.

The building is constructed mostly of cut-stone and granite, which I had trucked in from The Mesabi Range in Minnesota, and, Bianca Carrara marble, imported from Italy. The structural support for the main entrance, which is on the South side, and the lobby floor, were done with marble to symbolize the timeless beauty and endurance of the proclamation in The Pledge of Allegiance: "... and justice for all." Using marble as a small part of the overall architecture was, in my opinion, the proper thing to do. It signifies class and dignity and establishes respect...not for the rule of any royalty, autocrat or judge, but, for the idealism of true justice.

After visitors stroll through the garden and up the front steps, they will see, chiseled in the marble directly above the main entrance, the Latin words: "Lux et Veritas"...which means, translated to English: "Light and Truth."

And, after they proceed into the two-story, pristine lobby, they will see the gleaming sun beams passing through the many windows, some of which are stained-glass.

There are two busts displayed on pedestals in the lobby...one of Socrates and the other of Plato. I have put them there to honor their cogent reasoning and insistence that law and order must prevail for a society to achieve true freedom and democracy.

Easy access off the lobby to the courtroom is facilitated by two wide doors, and, even though there is usually a full-house for each session, there is seldom any congestion or disruption. The local building codes specify that doors, two on both sides, be available for emergency exit in case of fire or whatever, but, they are not used during normal operations. The restrooms are located in the hall on either side of the exit on the west side.

The seating of the spectators is efficiently handled by my security staff. Crowd control is a priority, but, most visitors, after spending time in the garden and the lobby, understand the significance of the upcoming proceedings and are cognizant of their expected conduct, so, a 'show of force' is rarely needed. Video surveillance ensures identification of anyone displaying questionable behavior and is regarded as a potential problem.

There is a roped-off section in the front-left of the wooden floor which is reserved for visiting guests and dignitaries, and, a small table for the steno. The general seating area is arranged with wooden pews in three sections separated by two aisles. My bench is front and center and is raised-up on a platform that is two feet above the main floor.

There is a small waiting room right off the courtroom on the east side where the accused on the day's docket are sequestered. They were brought in through the back door, to avoid any contact with the spectators. Under the watch of two guards, they will sit and ponder their destiny while they wait their turn to be escorted into the courtroom by Wilbur to a spot directly in front of my bench. Here, they will have one last say on their own behalf before they learn their fate.

The courtroom itself has a two-story high ceiling, and, there is a narrow balcony on two sides. A large crystal chandelier hangs from the center of the ceiling, but, it's dazzling array of lights are only needed on rare cloudy days. Most of the time the South Florida sun, shining through the side and back windows, provides ample light in the courtroom.

There is a short hallway inside the door which leads to my chambers, and, there are stairs off the hall that lead up to the second floor where the records room and a storage room are located.

My private entrance is in the back. The door is about twice the size of a normal door and is solid oak. It has two dead-bolt locks, and, because of it's bulk, it requires four large hinges for support that squeak under the stress of the door's weight when it's opened or closed.

Wilbur asked me once if I wanted him to spray some oil on the hinges to stop the squeak and I said, "No, I like it the way it is."

He looked at me out of the corner of his eye and said, "Whatever... are you serious?"

I laughed at him, but, I was serious...I like the sound. Sometimes, when I walk through that door, I pretend I am slowly opening a door to a medieval castle and entering the magical kingdom of King Arthur and his band of loyal knights. I even bought a suit-of-armor and stood it up at attention in the hallway right outside my chambers door to guard against knaves and rogue pillagers who might be roaming the nearby land.

I am responsible for having the courthouse built, but, it truly belongs to the people. I consider it a monument to American justice...a citadel that represents the brilliance of those who established the groundwork and the discipline. I know that traces of corruption and politics will always be ingrained in the legal system, as it is with any other segment of society. All I can do is strive to apply the law as it was intended.

THE START OF A FANTASTIC EVENING

YOU MIGHT BE wondering how it is that official legal proceedings may take place on my private property. You may ask why aren't there any ethical ramifications, hassles from the ABA or the judicial hierarchy as a result of me holding court literally in my back yard.

About ten years ago I began presiding behind the bench at the courthouse in the county seat. It was located in a small town, about 25 miles from where I now live, that was a nice, quiet place to live and work, and, rear a family. For the first six months after I was seated, there were no major problems and everything at the courthouse and in town seemed to run as smoothly as could be expected and everyone got along just fine.

But, with my reputation in full bloom as a result of the Roth trial, there were people who wanted to sit and watch the action in my courtroom in person.

There began an increasing influx of visitors from all over the state and even from neighboring states. Families on vacation would make the courthouse one of their planned destinations along with Disney World, the beach or wherever. It seemed there was always someone taking pictures or video of their kids standing on the front steps or climbing the 10-foot statue of Ben Franklin that was located by the front walk. The parking lots and streets were jammed with cars, busses and RVs, and, there was never enough local police and security available to sufficiently control the crowds and the traffic.

Some of the other judges and staff were starting to get steamed about driving in to the courthouse every morning and finding their parking spots taken by out-of-towners. The noise created by these people who were, at times, standing in the halls and outside waiting to get into my courtroom while yelling at their kids to stop splashing in the drinking fountain or running foot-races through the halls, was becoming very annoying. And, the litter of hamburger wrappers, beer and pop cans and food strewn all over the front lawn everyday, along with the lack of enough restroom facilities, was starting to concern the Sanitation Department.

There were a couple judges who got a little envious, it seemed to me, and resented the attention I was starting to get. Honestly, even after the huge publicity bump I got after the Roth trial, I did not expect all this to happen and I felt very uncomfortable with the unwanted notoriety.

The genesis of the inspiration for my courthouse occurred on a beautiful Friday afternoon. I had just finished cleaning up some last-minute paperwork in my office after a long day on the bench and was ready to head home and take the dogs for a run on the beach. I was making sure I had my keys before I closed the door on the way out when Jenny, the Clerk-of-Courts, happened to be walking by, and, she said, "Hi there, Judge Ed, what's up?"

Before I could answer, she said, "Judges Howard and Hardy and I are going across the street to The Jury Bar for a beer, why don't you come on over and join us?"

She was cute, single and had a great pair of legs and I always admired her because she was very good at her job. She took no grief from anyone. I never had any chances to have a casual chat with her since we were both busy and our paths seldom crossed. When we did speak, it was usually...sign this...check that, so, I thought, what the heck, I don't think I want to pass up an opportunity like this... the dogs can wait.

I said, "Okay, Jenny, that sounds good to me, and, please, just call me Ed."

She smiled and said, "You got it...Ed."

She said she had to go down to her office to pick up her jacket and she would meet me out front and we could walk over together. I said OK.

Just before locking the door I saw my cell phone lying on my desk. I grabbed it, closed the door and headed down the steps.

I wasn't outside more than three minutes when she came bouncing out the door and said, "Here I am...sorry to keep you waiting."

We walked across the street to the bar and sat down at the table with Howard and Hardy, who were already on their second beer. I liked them and respected them as good, honest judges, and, I think they liked me, so, we got along and had fun.

We engaged in the usual shop-talk with a few dirty jokes mixed in. Jenny laughed right along with us and she wasn't afraid to offer her opinions once in a while. She even told a joke, which I thought was the funniest one of the day. Just getting to know her a little bit that afternoon made me realize she had her act together.

I told the story about some chump who recently appeared in my courtroom on charges of cruelty to animals and being a public nuisance.

It went something like this:

This guy had a pet duck, which was very loud and obnoxious, and, he used it, as he put it, as a "guard dog" for his property. He kept the duck, named Heathcliff, tied up in his front yard so it could let him know, by it's loud, incessant quacking, if anyone was approaching his house. I guess he actually rigged-up a harness for it that was attached to a rope which was tied to a tree.

The problem was that it squawked at not only strangers who walked up to the front door, but, also, all the neighbors, people walking on the sidewalk, delivery persons, the gas and electric meter-readers and even cars driving by his house. This went on all day and most the night. The paper boy refused to deliver the paper to the front porch anymore and began throwing it from the sidewalk. He wasn't very accurate, as it landed, most of the time, in the flowers or bushes. The letter carrier tied up the mail in a bundle with a rubber-band and tossed it up the driveway and kept walking to the next house.

The neighbors claimed that very seldom was there any water or food made available for the poor duck, which was confirmed by the two officers who finally went to the house in response to a boatload of complaints that had been called in and filed over the last several weeks. They had indicated that there was no food, the water bowl was almost empty and the ground around the tree was covered with feces. And, the owner had ignored numerous warnings mailed to him by the police department concerning the horrible treatment of the duck and the disturbances it was causing.

Hardy slammed his beer down on the table and said, "He's the one that should be tied up with no water or food."

"Amen to that," agreed Howard.

Once, a pizza delivery boy walked up the steps to the front door unaware of the duck. Just as he rang the doorbell, the duck, which was awakened from a snooze in the bushes next to the steps, leaped out yakking and squawking, with wings flapping, and tried to take a bite out of the kid's leg. He was so startled that he screamed, jumped up and then fell backwards into the bushes. The top of the pizza box popped open and slices of pepperoni and sausage pizza went flying out all over the front yard.

Well, when this guy finally shows up in my courtroom to face the music, I became disgusted with his flippant attitude as he stood before me and made his feeble plea for leniency.

Before I handed down his sentence, I told him, "If this was the army, I would have you shot at sunrise."

He came back, "But, ya' couldn't do that, yer Judgeship."

I said, "Why not?"

"Because I don't get up that early."

Considering the mood I was in, I was surprised that I laughed out loud along with everyone else in the courtroom. I'm still not sure if he was serious or not, but, it didn't matter, it made me laugh. It actually was a welcome respite from a long day.

I quickly brought the courtroom back to order with a few wraps of my gavel and then issued him his marching orders.

They were: $1,000 fine, $250 in court costs and 30 days in the slammer. However, the jail time would be suspended contingent upon me receiving valid documentation of his working 100 hours as a volunteer at the local humane society.

Jenny asked, "What happened to the duck?"

I said I thought the humane society kept it a few days to make sure it was back in good health and then released it on a lake somewhere nearby.

She said, "As nasty as it was, I'm sure it won't have any trouble surviving out there."

Then, Judge Howard told an amazing story about a woman, who was scheduled for trial the next week, requesting a very unique plea-bargain agreement in his chambers and we all laughed and said some people will do just about anything to avoid the long arm of the law.

We had been there for almost two hours and the time was right, I guess, for things to wind down. They all finished their last beer and said it was time to get going. Everyone was leaving town for the weekend and they thought it best to hit the road before they got too hammered. I was hoping that Jenny would stick around a little longer, but, no such luck...maybe next time.

WHAT DID YOU SAY?

HE PLACE WAS starting to get crowded and I didn't want to sit at the table by myself, so, I got up and started to weave my way over to the bar. The beer was tasting pretty good so I thought I would finish this one and then drink one more before I left...the dogs could wait a little longer.

As I stood at the end of the bar waiting for the bartender to notice me, some guy sitting on a stool next to me tapped me on the shoulder and said, "There's an empty stool over here if you want to sit down, but, you better do it fast, I think the guy in the red shirt over there is lookin' this way and he's probably thinkin' about sittin' here."

It sounded like a good idea, so, I walked around and sat down next to him. He was young and seemed like a nice guy. I looked at him and said, "Thanks," as I was grappling for some money in my pocket. The bartender finally spotted me and walked over to find out what I wanted. I told him to get me a Rolling Rock and also get the fellow next to me whatever he was drinking...I think it was a Stroh's.

After he went to get the beer, the guy sticks his hand out and says, "Hi, my name is Wilbur and thanks for the beer."

I shook his hand and replied, "Hi, Wilbur, my name is Ed and you're welcome."

As we both sat and waited for our beers I noticed he kept looking at me like he recognized me. He'd look away for a moment and then glance back at me, and, finally said, "I'm sorry, I don't mean to be rude and stare, but, I think I know you. I get the feeling I've seen you before. I think maybe I've seen your picture in the paper or something...let's see...oh, heck...oh...I got it!...you're that Judge Ed guy. That's who you are. You're really famous. Wow, you sure have caused quite a stir around these parts."

"I guess I have," I said, as the bartender smacked down two beers in front of us. I gave him some money and then we both grabbed the bottles and took a drink. The beer was always very cold here, which was why I liked the place.

Wilbur continued; "You know, I usually try not to pay much attention to what's goin' on around town...you know...just work my job, come in here once in a while and throw-down a few beers and then go home. But, lately it's kinda been hard not to notice all the confusion and congestion...people getting in fights over stupid stuff, and, hearing all kinds of nasty words flyin' around."

"My boss told me that city-council is planning to meet in some sort of special session next week to figure out what to do about all the traffic coming into town and all the people just hangin'-out in the streets, and, I guess it's all because of you."

I took another swig of my Rock and smiled while I listened to him assess the situation probably better than any newspaper reporter could.

"I work at Hank's Hardware Store down on the next block and I hear people all the time that come in there talkin' about how they're getting fed-up with the mess of people in town. There's even talk that some townies are threatenin' to organize a mob and march over to the mayor's office to try and get something done about it."

"Heck, just the other day, a big hunk of a woman wearin' an orange sweat-suit that had written on the front: "If You Want It... Try and Come and Get It", a white head-band and black high-top Nike's comes bargin' into the store lookin' to buy some shells for her shotgun."

"She was all worked-up. She said she'd had enough and was gonna blow some tires out on a few cars and RV's that were parked illegally and then "those damn intruders," as she put it, might think twice before they drive in here again and try to take over her town."

He paused, took a long drink, and, then, went on; "I said, hold on mama...you need to back-off a little bit and calm down. I bought her a Coke out of the machine in the back and told her to sit down by the air-conditioner and relax for a spell. Plus, I didn't want to sell her any ammo for her gun and be linked later on to this woman's crazy shootin' spree. Something obviously just happened to her down the street but there was no way I was gonna ask her about it because I was afraid she might try to shoot me for wantin' to talk about it."

I laughed.

"I even heard the mayor on the radio yesterday sayin' that the Highway Patrol and police from other townships can't help with crowd control because something about the courthouse being within the city limits so it's out of their jurisdiction. He said not to worry, that they would work out a solution. Right, like I really believe that."

I said, "Yeah...well...I hope somebody comes up with something soon. Heck, just driving in to town everyday is becoming a stupid hassle. My chauffeur is tired of running the tires over the feet of people who crowd out into the streets and pound the windows when we drive by. I finally wised-up and stopped doing the limo thing, though. Now, I put on a fake beard and hat and drive my pick-up into town and I can usually get past them without being noticed. If it wasn't for the security chain I hung across the driveway in back of the courthouse, I wouldn't be able to pull in my parking space. Sometimes, I feel like Frankenstein being chased around by all those crazed villagers. Next thing they're gonna do is light up some torches and storm the courthouse."

"I think I saw that movie," Wilbur replied, "That poor dude did have a bad time."

He took another drink of his Stroh's and, then, after a short pause while he checked out a cute girl that had brushed against him as she walked by, said, "Heck, judge...now don't get me wrong...I don't like to tell other people how to run their business, but, if I were you, I'd build my own damn courthouse. Build it somewhere out in the country where you got some space. You could control the people better and there would be no collateral damage to the town. Everybody would be happy again, and, it would be your show."

I choked on the chug of beer I had just swallowed and started gasping for air. I was jolted by what I had just heard and I started coughing and gagging. I was desperately trying to gain back some composure while people close by were glancing over to see what was wrong with me. Wilbur started patting me on the back and kept asking if I was okay. I couldn't speak yet...so, I nodded.

After a few minutes, I was able to start breathing normally again and I grabbed a napkin off the bar to mop the tears that were filling up my eyes, and, some beer that had gotten up in my nasal cavity and was starting to dribble out of my nose.

I was blind-sided by the utter brilliance of Wilbur's suggestion. I realized then that there were going to be some dramatic changes in my life coming soon and a new dream envisioned because of what he had just said.

SO LONG... BUT, KEEP IN TOUCH

WILBUR SAT BACK down on the stool and said he was glad that I was okay. He was not aware of the impact his words just had on me. He thought beer had drained down the wrong pipe because I drank it too fast.

The fact was, I had just experienced a sudden and almost cathartic surge that had caused me to gag on my beer and become dazed for a few moments. When my head cleared again and I regained my senses, I felt energized.

Now, I had to get moving...I couldn't sit any longer, there was too much stuff churning around in my head, so, I told Wilbur I was ready to leave. He said he was ready, too. We gulped down the rest of our beer, I tipped the bartender and then we headed for the front door.

When we got outside, Wilbur and I shook hands and said goodbye. I asked him if he needed a ride home or to his car, and, he said no thanks, he had parked his car behind the hardware store, where he always does, and it was just a short walk.

As he started to walk away, I blurted out, "Hey, Wilbur, it was nice to meet you. You'll never know how enjoyable my time with you was in there. Maybe I'll see you again sometime."

He stopped and turned around and reached in his shirt pocket. He pulled out a business card and handed it to me.

"Here, take this, I got lots of 'em. The store prints 'em out for me because sometimes I do deliveries and sales work on the road. My home and work numbers are on there so you can call me whenever you want. I don't have a cell phone but I'm lookin' to get one soon. I can't afford one right now with my car payments and rent and everything, but, I'm suppose to get a raise soon and then maybe I can get one."

As I took the card from him and started to put it in my wallet I noticed some guy, who looked like a reject from the '70's but without the bell-bottoms, standing by the front window glaring at me and acting like he might recognize me or whatever, so, I thought I better get moving. I think Wilbur sensed that I was getting a little nervous with all the people milling around out front on the patio, so, he waved and said, "I'm outta here."

As he turned and stepped down off the curb and began to cross the street, totally oblivious to the on-coming traffic, he looked back at me and shouted, "I had a good time too, judge...see ya'."

As I started to walk the other way, I heard someone laying on their horn. I looked back to see what was happening, and, before I could yell at Wilbur to watch out, a flat-bed truck carrying a load of watermelons, that was speeding down the inside lane, swerved just in time and barely missed squashing him all over the front grill like a giant bug. The quick, evasive maneuver by the truck driver caused some of the melons to roll off and smash on the pavement. One of them landed right by Wilbur and splattered all over his pants and shoes. He jumped back on the curb, shook his feet a few times in an attempt to get the seeds and chunks of rind off his loafers, took a deep breath and said, "Well, I guess I'll walk down to the light and cross."

I hollered, "Yeah...that would be a good idea. Are you sure you're okay?"

He unconvincingly muttered, "No problem, judge...everything is under control."

Even though he tried to play it off, I could tell he was still a little shook up from his close encounter with the truck as he jitter-bugged his way down the sidewalk toward the intersection.

Before he got to the corner he had inadvertently bumped into an elderly man who had stopped momentarily to adjust his suspenders, and, he about knocked over a woman who was carrying a large bag of groceries and caused a six-pack of soda cans to fall out and slam on the sidewalk popping one open and squirting Mountain Dew all over her shoes.

All of a sudden it flashed in my mind...the things I've seen this guy do out here in such a short period of time, could he be the second-coming of Chief Inspector Clouseau?

I waited and watched as he finally got safely to the other side of the street and then I headed for my pick-up.

I knew the dogs would be upset wondering where I was...pacing...panting...watching...waiting for me to show up. I needed to get home and out on the white sand with them to think this whole thing out. I needed to start formulating a plan. I knew one thing for sure, when Wilbur mentioned building the courthouse "somewhere out in the country," I had no doubts as to where that "country" would be...it would be my property.

I also was fairly confident that Wilbur was going to fit somehow in the grand scheme of things, but, I needed to focus on the immediate task at hand, which was devising my strategy to gain approval for the construction of my own courthouse.

MAKING IT HAPPEN

AFTER ARRIVING HOME, I went up to the bedroom and put on a pair of shorts, a T-shirt and sandals. I stopped by the kitchen to grab a tuna sandwich and then went out to let the dogs loose. They had been yapping (as they usually do) ever since they saw me pull the truck up to the garage. They knew they were about to be let out of their pen and were letting me know it was about time I showed up to do it. I heard about it the entire time I was in the house.

Once I went back out the door and started walking toward them their anticipation intensified. I tried to talk calmly to them and let them know I was on the way, but, it did no good...they were on a roll.

The instant I opened the gate to their pen, my knees got slammed as all three busted out and sprinted directly across the parking area, like race horses coming out of the starting gate, and, over to the pathway that leads down to the beach. Before I could get the gate closed and latched they had disappeared...the sound of their constant barking gradually fading as they neared the water.

By the time I got down to the beach, they had already found their favorite stick and had dropped it in the sand right in front of where they were standing and waiting. With their tails wagging at top speed, they were staring at me with the look of like...'well...what took you so long to get here and why are you just standing there looking at us?'

I apologized to them for my slowness in arriving and for being so inconsiderate, and, then, I picked up the stick.

Now, things changed in a hurry. Their tails immediately froze and were sticking straight out as all three of them became like statues with their eyes riveted on the stick in my hand knowing the moment they had been waiting for all day was finally here. I reached back and made a huge motion like I was throwing it down the beach toward the water, but, I didn't let go.

They took off sprinting through the sand at full speed and were looking up and all around to see where the stick was going to come down. After running around in circles a few times and jumping in the water trying to find it, they all three stopped, as if on cue, and looked back down the beach at me and saw me waving the stick in the air. They realized they had been had. They came charging back up the beach barking at me to let me know they were not happy with my little joke. (they fall for it every time) Then, just as they were coming to a sliding stop at my feet, I hurled it way down the beach this time and they made a quick U-turn and were off and running again.

How I treasure my time with my dogs...what great friends and companions they are.

As I continued hurling the stick, my mind began to shift gears back to the 'think' mode. I considered all the possible angles of approach for my new endeavor, and, tried to formulate the most viable strategy I could use to make my courthouse a reality. I also knew there would be the inevitable headaches of such an undertaking, but, it didn't matter...I knew, whatever the hurdles would be, I was going to do everything I could to make it happen.

Finally, after an hour or so, the heat was starting to take it's toll and the dogs had reached near exhaustion. Their tongues were practically dragging in the sand now, and, so, it was into the water for some cooling off. The surf was the perfect temperature for an absolute refreshing plunge.

But, we were dehydrated, so, I told them it was time to start heading back up to the house to get some water.

As we walked up the path, enjoying the welcome shade the palm trees and tall shrubs provided, I determined that the absolute necessity of the courthouse and the proposal I had just decided to present to the city-council would far outweigh any potential harmful consequences or the possibility of setting a bad precedent. And, I was convinced this would also be apparent to The State Judicial Board, which would ultimately make the final decision. I also figured someone along the way was bound to come up with something like... "Well, if we allow this to happen, then, another judge will want to do the same thing somewhere else."

The problem with that reasoning is that there may be another judge who would want to build his/her own courthouse, but, the fact is, there is no other judge who needs to. Therein lies the difference and I knew that would be a determining factor in their decision.

It can be a reality...it will be a reality. Why not? This entire scenario has only one logical conclusion. How could anyone not agree that it is the sensible thing to do considering the turmoil occurring almost daily in town?

So, with my proposal in hand and a confident and positive attitude, I went and made my pitch at the monthly city council meeting. Then, I appeared a week later before The State Committee on Jurisdiction of Courts, which is the zoning branch of The State Judicial Board. There was the predictable grumbling from one or two members of both panels, but, overall, I thought it went good and they were very receptive.

The police reports and analyses of the increase in criminal activity and arrests in and around town over the last two years were, as one board member put it, "eye-opening." A comparison of the approved city budget for the past two years and the actual money that has been appropriated for overtime pay for officers, security personnel, EMTs, maintenance and sanitation crews, etc., which had depleted the city coffers down into the red zone, was also a direct hit.

And, since polls seem to be the newest trend in swaying public opinion, I presented the results of a poll that was taken of 92% of all adult citizens in the district which showed that 89% of them were in favor of Judge Ed getting the hell out of town. The fact that they were "eligible voters" seemed to have prompted the mayor to sit up and pay closer attention.

It took about three weeks for both the city council and the judicial committee to approve the transfer of my court to a new venue located on my land. However, they made it perfectly clear that the jurisdiction would still be the same as it was in town, and, it would also be contingent on me providing 80% of the funding for the construction and supplying all security and traffic control. That was fine with me because I had already anticipated that responsibility.

The final piece of the puzzle was the okay from the state board, and, when that happened it was full speed ahead.

WILBUR

A S CONSTRUCTION WAS in progress on the courthouse, I spent most of my spare time organizing and preparing the logistics of the security and parking that would have to be in place when the spectators started showing up on opening day. I knew they would come and I had to make sure everything was on schedule, all operations fully tested and all security personnel screened with background checks, trained and ready to work as a team.

But, I still needed someone to be my personal aide and a 'do-it-all' kind of guy in the courthouse and around the residential complex. Someone I could trust and who was a good worker. To find such a person, I knew I would have to come up with some sort of strategy. I might need to get a list of names and recommendations from colleagues at the courthouse, and, then, interview and evaluate...not something I was eager to do.

Or, I could hire an employment agency, but, if I did, I would be too removed from the process. I wanted to be more involved than just turning my search over to some desk jockeys who had no idea how to sense the intangibles and character of the man for whom I was looking.

But, the bonus was, I had already met him. It was so obvious, but, it just didn't click.

Then, one night, I was cleaning up my desk at home and I found the business card that Wilbur had given to me the night we first met at The Jury Bar. My mind had been occupied by many things recently and my intention to call him had been subconsciously shoved to the back of my brain, out of the way, to make room for other stuff. Finding the card made me realize I had forgotten what my instincts had told me right after we said goodbye outside the bar that night. Even though he almost got splattered by a watermelon truck, he could be the guy who fit the job description best.

I was going to get in touch with him to see if he has been successful in avoiding any more self-destructive incidents or encounters, and, if so, what was going on in his life. (After all, he certainly changed mine) I assumed he was still working at the hardware store and I wanted to persuade him to meet me for a beer at The Jury Bar one day after work. I remembered that he liked Stroh's, so, I figured it shouldn't be too hard to convince him to drink a couple cold ones with me. I didn't want to tell him over the phone that I was offering him a job...I thought it would be better if I did that in person.

Wilbur had lived a helter-skelter life as young boy. His dad was a Marine sergeant who traveled from one training camp to another as a drill instructor, training commander and advisor. He had a revered reputation as a man who commanded (not demanded) respect and admiration from officers and enlisted men for his expert knowledge and skills in searching for and destroying terrorists on the ground.

Wilbur and his mom usually tagged along with him when he was transferred back and forth across the country, and, they lived in various military housing units, some of which were not very comfortable or conducive for rearing children. They never stayed long enough in one place for Wilbur to settle in, make any friends or get into the flow of things in school, so, he never had a legitimate chance to achieve his potential.

He had no brothers or sisters so he was very close to his mother since they were the only two around the house most of the time. She was morally strong and very loving, and, he grew up with the proper discipline and guidance. And, even though his dad was gone a lot, his mother made sure that he understood that his father was serving his country and he should always be proud of his commitment and bravery.

During those rare days when his dad was home, he was always with Wilbur and enjoyed joking around and making him laugh. He would help him with his homework and they would shoot baskets at the park...anything they felt like doing...as long as they were together.

Wilbur never forgot the one night at the dinner table when his dad said how he was happiest when he was with Wilbur and his mom, and, that "happiness is the most important thing to have in life." Wilbur couldn't help but think this to be true since he was always happiest when he was with him.

They made the most of their limited time together and Wilbur thought he was the luckiest boy in the world to have a father like him.

Wilbur loved his mother and father very much.

Then, when the hostilities increased in the Middle East, his dad was sent to Iraq to serve in Desert Storm, where he gave his life by falling on a live grenade, that had been booby-trapped by a terrorist insurgent, to save the lives of the other marines in his squad.

Wilbur was 15 years old when his father died and the mega-shock of his death caused his whole world to collapse around him. His mother did her best to deal with her sorrow and still be strong enough to offer the support that Wilbur needed, but, she couldn't continually maintain her mental toughness. Her grief was so powerful, it was slowly eating her away on the inside.

After about a year, she began to drink because of her increasing inability to deal with the loneliness and depression. It got worse and worse. Wilbur took care of her and encouraged her, but, his love and devotion could not overcome her lack of desire to live anymore. The pain of seeing her wither away right in front of his eyes was devastating to him. A lot of people would have given up, but, Wilbur was of strong character and will and never left his mothers side.

His dad received 'The Medal of Honor' posthumously, which is the highest honor that can be bestowed upon any military man or woman.

His entire combat squad, whose lives were saved by his heroic act, sergeants from four other squads and the 3-star Commander of the troops in Iraq at that time, flew in to the town where they were living, drove to their house with a police escort and presented the medal and The American Flag, which was draped over the coffin at his funeral and burial in Arlington National Cemetery, to his mother, with a salute, along with a letter written and signed by The President of the United States, which stated, in part, "... myself and all Americans will forever be indebted to your husband for his bravery and ultimate sacrifice for the freedom of our great country."

Wilbur still has all three items, which he said he will "always cherish." His mother gave them to him just before she died.

Wilbur was 18 when he buried his mother. And, on that day, he took a vow to dedicate his life to the memory of his parents by joining The Marines right after he graduated from high school, which would be two months from then. He wanted to be the man that his dad was and this was the way he could do it. And, it made him feel good inside knowing his mom and dad would be proud of him.

The day after he graduated he went to the nearest recruiting office. When he walked in the door he felt a surge of emotion that made him realize that this was, indeed, the right thing to do. And, he knew his dad and mom were with him as he walked up to the desk where a man in full dress uniform had just stood up and extended his hand to welcome him..

But, his dream was shattered in a short time. He was rejected because of his admission on the physical exam application that he had asthma, which he developed as a child. He never considered this malady to be a problem because he periodically took medication, along with using his inhaler, that kept it under control. But, it still prevented him from entering military service.

The staff-sergeant who had to tell Wilbur he could not be a Marine, did so with tears in his eyes because he knew of his father's reputation and heroic deed, and, how badly Wilbur wanted to follow in his foot-steps.

For a few weeks after that day, he was depressed and confused and didn't do much of anything. He wandered through malls, went to movies and sat on a bench in the public park trying to come up with a reason why his life changed so fast. He was now adrift in the world all alone and he needed to try to make some sense out of his newly arranged existence. It wasn't so much a matter of salvaging his life, but, rather determining the direction it would take.

And, as he sat on a stool at the local pub about every night drinking beer, his determination to make something out of himself continued to get stronger. Unlike some of those lost souls lined up down the length of the bar who were slumped over their half-drank beer and empty shot glasses, he was not a quitter. At this point in time, life was presenting him with his biggest challenge right smack in the face and there was no getting out of the way.

He began to realize why his dad always told him to get right back up when you get knocked down and face the challenges that were awaiting him in life with courage...that he should always have faith in himself and be confident. He started to understand the wisdom of his dad's words and that their intent was to prepare him for a moment just like this.

If he couldn't be a Marine, then, even with no college degree, he would get the best job possible and be a success. He just had to get up off his duff and go do it.

So, with the money he received from the settlements of his parents will and insurance, and, the Benevolent Fund of The Marine Corps., he bought a used car that was in much better condition than the one he was driving, loaded up all of his belongings he could get in the car and decided to head South.

He drove down to South Florida in hopes of getting a job doing some construction work and rehab on houses that were damaged or destroyed by a hurricane that blew through the area a month earlier. He wanted to make enough money so he could rent a decent place to live.

He pounded nails for a while, but, found out that he wasn't getting the money he should have because he wasn't a "dues-paying" member of the local construction union. Even though there was a shortage of workers to tackle the massive rebuilding that needed to be done, Wilbur was told he would get only part-time wages, so, he started looking for another job.

He lived in run-down motels while he worked odd jobs as he traveled from one town to another for the next year or so. He did everything from painting houses to putting up billboard signs, but, was constantly looking for a better job...anything that would help improve his life.

Then, he landed a job at a hardware store after seeing a "help-wanted" sign in the window. And, since the store happened to be in the same town where the courthouse was located...well...the rest is history.

Out of curiosity, I went to visit the owner and manager of Hank's Hardware Store to get his take on Wilbur and his work habits. Wilbur had been there for over three years so I figured he could give me a valid appraisal.

He knew who I was after I introduced myself and was very cordial. He offered me some coffee and showed me a picture, which was hung on the wall behind the register, of his dad holding him as a baby in one arm and their dog in the other, standing in front of the store 47 years earlier when it first opened for business.

He claimed to have sat in my courtroom three times to watch a high-profile trial that I presided over a couple months ago. He said he was "cheering" for me the whole time and that the "low-life" got what he deserved. I felt a little embarrassed by his compliment, but, I'm always glad to hear comments from people who enjoyed their visit in court.

He then went on to tell me things about Wilbur that just reinforced what I was thinking all along... that he was the guy for the job.

I called him the next night, and, when I told him it was me, he seemed shocked. It had been almost a year since we met and he was surprised that I called. As he put it...why would "such a busy man" take the time to call him?

We talked for a while and agreed to meet at The Jury Bar after he got off work the next Monday. I jokingly reminded him to cross the street at the light when he walked over from the store.

He laughed and said, "I always do, judge...I learned my lesson."

I arrived first and sat at the end of the bar. I ordered a Rolling Rock and told the barmaid that a friend was coming to meet me and when he got here to bring him a Stroh's.

I was almost finished with my beer when he finally showed up. He apologized for being late. He explained that the store had a big rush of customers right at closing time and he had to stay a little longer than normal to make sure everyone got what they needed, and, then, he helped the owner sweep the floor and close up.

He looked in good health and I noticed his arms and shoulders seemed a little more muscular than I remembered. I mentioned to him that he was starting to look like Mr. America and that he must be eating his spinach. He laughed and said he didn't like spinach, but, he does work out three times a week at the Y because he thinks pumping iron and running makes him feel better and have more energy. I agreed.

The barmaid promptly brought over his Stroh's and another Rock for me.

After we both took a swig, I made my offer to him. He reacted in amazement, disbelieving that I would want him to be the one to accept this position that came with so much responsibility. I reminded him that it was his idea to build my own courthouse and he should, therefore, be a part of it's operation. He gradually realized that I was serious and so he said he would give it a try.

I said, "Good, I know you'll do a good job."

We briefly discussed some of his basic duties, but, I didn't want to overwhelm him right off the bat...there would be more time later to fill him in on salary, hours and everything else he needed to know. The key was getting him to accept my offer. I also reminded him to make sure he alerted the store owner about the situation to allow him enough time to find a suitable replacement.

Hiring Wilbur turned out to be the best decision I could have made. He always does whatever he is suppose to do (well...most of the time), and, he usually does a little extra, also. And, even though he couldn't be a Marine, I know his mom and dad would be proud of him for the way he has conducted his life and grown to be a good man.

I've learned over the years to always expect the unexpected from Wilbur.

Like the time I made sun-tea.

I set the covered glass jar full of water and two tea bags on the pool deck in the sun so it would be ready for when I ate lunch, which would be about an hour later, and, then, dove in the water to swim my daily laps. About five minutes into my swim, as I was doing a turn at the end of the pool, I noticed Wilbur had come out of the house and picked up the glass jar and set it on the table. I stopped and asked him why he did that and he said, "I wanted to get it closer to the sun so it will brew faster for you."

The sun is 93 million miles away and he wanted to put it three feet closer.

I can only laugh and enjoy Wilbur at his best.

I treat him like my own son now, and, I have adopted him as my ward.

I've grown to love him, but, I hesitate to tell him because I think it would pale in comparison to the love he knew from his mother and father. I think he knows how I feel, but...I guess some things are best left unspoken.

JENNY

WAS HOPING THAT tonight would blossom into a fantastic time for Jenny and me, but, I didn't want to get my expectations up too high. I knew how I felt about her and how I wanted this evening to open up a new road to a true relationship...one like I've never had with any other woman.

Maybe such a desire was not possible. Maybe I wanted to live in a fantasy world and believe that an ideal match would just 'happen' without playing some hybrid form of the mating game with no guarantee that I would be able to figure out the rules before the game was over. It would probably wash up on the rocks and break apart before it ever had a chance to work. I've been through that before and I always came away with doubts about my ability to sustain a meaningful relationship.

Nevertheless, I was going to try to find out tonight if she had the potential to feel the same way about me as I did about her, and, then, go from there. But, the important thing for me to keep in mind was that there is no hurry...just let it flow along it's own course...at it's own pace. Don't rush it.

Back in the days when I was holding court at the county courthouse, when we would occasionally bump into each other during the course of our duties, I would always get a charge out of seeing Jenny. My pulse would bump up a couple of notches when she would see me in the hall and say, with a smile, "Hey, there, Judge Ed...how's business?"

And, the afternoon when we had a chance to talk over a few beers at The Jury Bar, with Judges Howard and Hardy sitting right across the table listening in on everything, I really couldn't take advantage of the situation and get anything going with her. But, I had witnessed enough of her charm to know that I definitely wanted to get to know her better.

Jenny had been to my house before for a few cocktail parties that I had hosted for some friends from the courthouse. I didn't have parties often and they were small in attendance, but, I always made sure that I asked Jenny if she could be there. She mixed well with whomever showed up because that was the way she was...easy to talk to, vibrant and innocently charming.

But, the real reason I invited her was because I wanted to be near her for an extended period of time and just see how everything would go, and, try to get a sense of our compatibility.

Sometimes, when we both had a chance to break away from the guests, we would sneak off to the kitchen for a while and maybe joke about which guest was wasted so bad they were acting like an alien from another galaxy that had just landed on Earth, or, laugh about some guy who had been trying to sneak a peek down her blouse. But, our time alone didn't last long. We both knew we had to get back to the action before they would start to wonder where we were.

Tonight, however, she would be here by herself.

How this highly anticipated night with her came about was because I half-joked with her one late afternoon, when we coincidentally met at the bottom of the stairs by the front door as we were leaving the courthouse, about coming over some Saturday or Sunday for a swim and some dinner. I guess I was casting a line in the water to see if I could get a nibble...see what her initial reaction would be. I was even going to offer to have my chauffeur pick her up, but, I stopped myself. I thought better because I didn't want to seem snobbish or come across as pushy in a blatant attempt to influence her decision.

I thought she would just say that she would think about it, or, she was seeing someone else right now, or, some other excuse. But, I was surprised when, without hesitation, she smiled and said, "I'd love to, Ed."

I was trying to stay cool.

She gave me her cell number and said to call her and let her know what day would be best for me and then she would let me know if it was good for her.

That was on a Tuesday, and, even though I was all for getting together that Saturday, I didn't call her until the next Monday because I didn't want to seem like I was too anxious and come across as a desperate man.

She really acted like she was glad to hear my voice when she answered. We talked for a few minutes about a disturbance that had occurred the previous Friday in the lobby of the courthouse when a potential juror, who was on break from a jury selection interview, screamed to a defendant who was being led through the hallway by a sheriff to a pre-trial hearing: "I can tell you're guilty as sin just by looking at you...they should throw you in a deep hole and forget you even exist."

The inmate jerked around and yelled, "Well, maybe I'll make it worth my time in that hole and just strangle your scrawny neck right here."

He lunged at the woman and tried to grab her but his leg shackles prevented him from moving quick enough. The crowd of people standing nearby in the lobby were startled by the sudden outburst and jumped back out of the way not knowing what to expect. But, the officer and a security guard were able to tackle him and zap him with the stun gun, and, then, drag him back to his cell before any damage was done. Needless to say, the woman was removed from the potential jury pool.

We both laughed and agreed that it had been sort of dull around the courthouse lately and the place needed a little excitement to finish off the week.

Then, I asked her, "How about coming over this Saturday?"

She replied, "That would be great."

"How about around three o'clock?", I said.

"Sounds good...see you then."

She arrived around 3:10. I had been working in and out of the house most of the day...doing some organizing and cleaning the pool. But, I made sure I wasn't doing something that would cause me to miss her when she pulled in the parking area from the road. The dogs were right outside the door barking at me. I knew what they wanted but I told them to back off...I would get to them as soon as I could.

I finally saw her car through the window as she coasted in from the road, across the compound and then stopping in front of the guest house.

I told the dogs to stay put on the porch and went out to greet her.

She hopped out of her car and said, "Hi, Ed." She was wearing jean shorts, a light green v-neck pull-over shirt and running shoes. Her light brown hair was beautiful in the sun.

"Welcome, Jenny, I'm really glad you could come."

She grabbed a tote bag from the back seat, which I assumed contained her swim suit and whatever, and, closed the door. She looked around with a puzzled look on her face, and, then said, "What's that noise?"

Then, she started to laugh when she saw my dogs sitting on the porch staring at us and whining loud enough for us to easily hear. I thought that it would be best if we went inside or they would keep up the moaning, so, I suggested we head over to the house.

As we were walking toward the porch she said, "Isn't it a beautiful day?"

Awesome. I was impressed that she said that to me. I admire a person who enjoys life to the fullest and are not afraid to express their appreciation for the splendidly simple things in life...like a beautiful day.

I agreed that it was indeed a gorgeous day, and, then, I told her how nice she looked. I don't know why I said it. I wasn't trying to score points right out of the chute or anything, it just kind of slipped out. My experiences with women have taught me that a well-timed compliment can sometimes make an evening go a little smoother, but, that's not why I said it. I guess I just inadvertently expressed what my heart felt before I could think of something else to say.

She blushed and said, "Thank you."

Then, I confessed that the dogs had been really bugging me about going down to the beach for their daily run, and, if I didn't take them soon they will probably tie me up to a tree and leave me for gator food... would she mind if we took them down for a little while?

She said, "What are we waiting for?"

All I had to say was, "Let's go," and the dogs were off like a shot down the path. She put her bag inside the front door and we hustled down after them. Before I could get to the stick, which was laying in front of them as they stood panting and waiting, Jenny jumped ahead of me, grabbed it off the sand and threw it a mile down the beach. Then, she yelled, "There you are...see if you can get that one."

She seemed very comfortable around them and they liked her, which was an encouraging sign because dogs can be a good judge of character. They ran up to her with the stick more often than they came to me. I could tell she was a very athletic girl by just watching her run and throw. When I mentioned to her that she looked like a natural athlete, she said, "No...not really, I'm not very good." I knew she was being modest.

Then, she told me she played softball and basketball in high school. That didn't surprise me...my guess was that she was a hell of a competitor.

When we got back to the house, I told her I was going up to my bedroom to put on my swim trunks and I would meet her back in the kitchen. She grabbed her bag and went to the downstairs bathroom to change. When we both got back to the kitchen I poured two glasses of lemonade and we walked out to the pool and relaxed on a couple lounge chairs. The sun was on full blast, so, at her suggestion, we jumped in the water. The dogs started running back and forth, barking and carrying on, and, letting me know that they didn't like the fact that we were in the water, but, they were not. (I don't allow them in the pool at certain times. I have explained to them occasionally, as they sat before me intently listening to every word, that there are times when they are not permitted in the pool, but, it goes in one ear and out the other) One of them even ran out on the diving board like he was going to do a front flip into the water. I finally yelled at all three to go get a drink of water out of their bowls, and, then, lie down in the shade somewhere and give it a rest.

Dinner on the veranda, looking out over the gulf at the beautiful sunset, was perfect and our attraction for each other seemed to flourish the longer we were together. We talked and laughed about everything and anything over boiled lobster and baked potatoes. She was bright and funny, and, seemed to be a lively mix of all the qualities a man would want in a good woman. My gut feeling was that, so far, things were moving along in the right direction.

After we finished eating, she took the dishes to the kitchen, and, by the time she came back out, I had poured some wine. We sat underneath the large umbrella by the pool and enjoyed the wonderful gulf breeze while we continued to talk.

When we emptied the bottle, we went back inside to get one more out of my wine-chest located in the kitchen next to the microwave, but, I never had a chance to pull out the cork. As I walked around the island counter to get two clean glasses off the rack, she playfully bumped me as I went by. I set the bottle down on the counter, turned and looked in her beautiful blue eyes and warned her that assault and battery on a judge is a very serious crime.

She laughed and said, "I guess I better get myself a good lawyer."

Then, we gravitated toward each other as if pulled together by some mystical force. It was so easy to reach out and bring her to me.

As we stood in each other's arms, I could feel her heart beating against my pounding chest as our lips met softly. I could feel her passion seep into my body and explode a feeling in my heart I had no idea was possible.

While we held each other, it felt to me that inside my arms was the place she should be...the place she belonged...like her body was specifically molded to fit perfectly against mine.

We finally let loose of each other. She caught her breath and said, "Holy cow...you certainly know how to make a girl feel her oats...that kiss jolted me all the way down to the bottom of my toes."

"I recharged my batteries last night."

She laughed again.

Then, she said that she better get going...it was getting late. I don't think it was because she wasn't having a good time, but, I got the feeling she felt it would be best to shut it down for the night. She probably thought the same thing I did...don't be in a hurry.

I understood. It's exactly what I told myself before she got here... don't push it. I was happy just to be with her and close to her.

I walked with her out to her car and we held each other one more time.

"Thank you for a great day, Ed," she said.

"Your welcome, Jenny"

I didn't have any trouble speaking with her the entire night, but, now that she was leaving, my mouth started to become dry. I was hesitant to say something because I thought I might be unable to come up with the words to fit the moment.

When she opened the door and got in, I felt a weird rush starting to set in. It was like all the blood was draining through my body down to my feet. What the hell was going on? Why did I feel like 'Robbie the Robot' all of a sudden?

I said goodbye as she started her car and put it in gear.

I knew I would miss her as soon as she drove her car down the road and out of sight. I wanted to open the door, reach in, take her by the arm and pull her back out of the car and hold and kiss her one more time, but, my instincts told me no way. "Don't be a fool, jerk, that's not the way it works." It was out of the question to pull a stupid stunt like that.

She slowly pulled out and drove across the open compound, and, then, looked back at me and honked as she turned onto the road. I waved and she was gone.

A very severe thirst had crept into my mouth, so, I went back inside and grabbed a Rock out of the fridge. I walked over to the stairs, carefully avoiding all three dogs who were crashed-out on the cool tile floor in the hall, and climbed up to my observation tower. I needed to sit for a while and collect my thoughts. I needed to dissect what just happened, and, under the glorious canopy of the Milky Way was where I wanted to be.

I struggled to figure out why it seemed so easy to be with her... what were the reasons I felt so comfortable with her?

Were there some kinds of momentary stimuli that could have distorted my usual perception of reality and possibly interfered or altered the natural progression of my emotions?

Was it just there for both of us because it was "meant to be?"

It could be that we were lucky enough to find some sort of middle-ground, or, a comfort-zone, where nothing could go wrong. Or, maybe the planets were aligned in some sort of magical celestial configuration causing the desires of both of us to be drawn together and perfectly coincide.

I knew my rambling thoughts were turning incoherent. Whatever the rationale might be, I was starting to fade fast. It was time to crash, so, I headed back down the steps. By the time I reached my bedroom, my brain was ready to close down and I realized I wouldn't be able to come up with any answers tonight...maybe not ever. I would have to wait until the morning, and, then, think about all of this some more.

My last thought before I blacked-out was that probably it really didn't matter why it happened. It's ridiculous to even waste my time trying to analyze my evening with Jenny. It would be best if I just enjoyed the memory of our time together and know that there was more to come.

THE ESCAPE

BENJAMIN ROTH HAD been devising his plan of deception and revenge for years. He had plenty of time to focus on his mission of total retribution while he sat in his cell at a Florida State Prison for the last six and a-half years seething with hate. But, he was able to control his anger and channel his energy to performing his daily activities and duties as best he could. He became a model prisoner because he figured it was the best and quickest way to gain parole, and, then, begin his quest for my head.

However, he didn't expect to get transferred to a minimum-security facility as a reward for his good behavior and volunteer work in the health clinic.

He earned exemplar status and was well liked by the prisoners and guards for offering his services performing fix-up surgery on the inmates and screws who got slashed in the face with a shiv or beaten to a bloody mess from time to time. He was always there to help, and, even served as a counselor and mediator when disputes among the inmates would start to boil over.

He was surprised at the news he was getting moved to a different location, but, realized it might be the next step to eventual freedom.

As he climbed into the prison van that would take him to his new home and snapped on his seatbelt, he felt a twinge of optimism for the first time since the slam of my gavel signaled the end to his trial almost seven years ago. A new environment would help his morale. And, even though he knew it was still 18 years away from his goal, he was able to force a wicked sneer thinking about how sweet it will be to see me beg for mercy like he did when I asked him if he had any last words before hearing his sentence. And, then, while I was groveling in the dirt at his feet, he would finally experience the long-awaited satisfaction of bashing my skull and rendering my face unrecognizable. A gun would be too impersonal, he thought...he wanted more direct and physical involvement with my demise.

And, how ironic it would be that a man exalted and praised for his ability to create new faces from mangled ones will soon be doing just the reverse...converting a normal, healthy face into a bloody pulp.

After the huge, iron front gate slowly grinded open with a clank, the van drove down the exit ramp onto the two lane county road that ran parallel to the front of the prison and headed west. Roth was being transported, along with two other inmates, to a facility 115 miles away. It would be about a two hour drive, and, coincidentally, in the same direction to where my residential complex was located.

It was late at night and there was a full moon dominating the crystal-clear sky that lit up the landscape in an eerie glow. As he settled in for the trip and laid his head back on the head-rest, Roth peered out of the window at the beauty of the illuminated night and wondered if this strange serenity he was feeling might be an omen of good things to come.

Then, about 70 miles into the drive, on a secluded stretch of road, his hope became a reality.

As one of the guards, who was sitting shotgun, popped open another can of beer and the van was speeding around a sharp curve, a large Stag deer suddenly appeared and was standing in the middle of the road 50 feet away staring at the head-lights of the on-coming van. As soon as the driver saw the animal he panicked. He jerked the wheel and the van veered across the other lane and off the road. He never even stomped on the brakes as it smashed into a tree, then, glanced off and rolled over two times and came to rest on it's top. Everyone...the two other inmates, two guards and the driver were dead or almost dead...except Roth.

While hearing the muffled moans of two bodies breathing their last breath and feeling the warm blood that was squirting in his face from the severed neck of one inmate crumbled next to him, he was able to unhook the seat-belt that had saved his life by keeping him from smashing his head against the windshield at 60 mph like all the others who were not wearing a seat-belt.

He wiggled out from underneath the guard's body that was on top of him. Being careful to avoid the gushing blood and splintered femur that had punctured out of the guard's leg and was protruding like a sharpened knife, he crawled out of the busted side window. Reaching back inside, he took the revolver and some bullets from the holster-belt of the guard...he thought it might be a good idea to have a little protection. And, he also grabbed the flashlight that had popped out of the glove box during the crash, and, was lying next to the driver's body...this would also be good to have. Since he was permitted to wear street clothes for the trip, he had pockets in his pants in which to keep the pistol and ammo. Then, he hobbled into the woods and disappeared long before a passing motorist saw the wreckage and called 911.

As soon as the police showed up and determined that Roth was not in the van with the other bodies, they organized a small search party. But, by then, he had traveled far enough into the dense forest that the deputies had no chance to find him in the dark. They didn't bother calling for the bloodhounds because dogs weren't much help in these parts due to the presence of alligators and snakes. They spook very easily at the sight of a gator with his mouth wide open or a snake poised to strike, which usually causes them to lose their concentration and the scent in a hurry. So, they decided to wait until daybreak to resume the search.

Roth stayed on the move, only hiding in one place for no more than a day, and, was able to survive by eating insects and the meat of small animals he was able to snag, and, drinking water from streams. Fortunately for him, he did not need to fire the gun anytime at an animal that might have been in an attack mode, which could have exposed his location. The cops would know he had a gun after they searched the wreckage and discovered that the guard's pistol was missing, so, if he had to blow something away and the search patrol happened to be in the vicinity, they would know where he was.

He knew he couldn't hide too long in the woods because they would definitely keep looking for him until they found him. The best thing to do would be to somehow vanish into thin air by disguising himself and assimilating into a town he hoped wouldn't be too far away by now. He thought to himself, "All this walking around...hell, there had to be a damn town out here somewhere."

After almost two weeks of being on the move he knew they had to be closing in on him. Finally, when he was getting ready to catch a few hours of sleep on a huge log, he saw lights coming through the trees. He walked a little further to a clearing and saw the beautiful town about a half mile away. The gods were still looking after him, he thought.

He now had long hair and a beard, which was a good start to his charade. And, if he was going to squeeze back into civilization again, the first priority would be to get a change of threads. There was still a few hours left before the sun would come up, so, he started to sneak toward the town, staying under cover as best he could. Once he got there he began scavenging in the alleys and found a long, flannel coat in a dumpster he could wear over his torn and blood-stained clothes. Then, he could go to the Goodwill store without being noticed and buy a pair of pants, a couple shirts, shoes and a baseball cap using some of the money they gave him as a "going-away gift" before he left the prison.

(The warden told Roth just before he walked out of the door that it was a pleasure to have known him and he was "one of the best prisoners we've ever had here at our home." The money, as he explained, was a token of gratitude for his cooperation and help in the clinic and would make life a little bit easier for him at the new facility. Roth wasn't sure what he meant by that and he didn't ask... he always thought the guy was a little weird. But, whatever they wanted to give him...he would take. He figured a man of his stature and prominence deserved anything he could get.)

He went in the changing room and put on his new clothes. He liked what he saw when he checked out his new wardrobe in the mirror and felt like a new man. Then, to complete his disguise, he put on a pair of sun-glasses he bought at the drug store. No one could recognize him now.

With his new disguise in place, he started knocking on the doors of some businesses in town, and, in a couple days, landed a job painting cars and trucks at an auto shop. (they never asked him for an ID) The shop owner paid him in cash to avoid employee taxes, which was the perfect arrangement for Roth. He earned good money and there was no record of his employment on file. He requested to work weekends, if needed, to make some overtime pay, and, also, maybe get some off-days during the week so he could periodically make the drive to my courthouse.

He was staying at the YMCA, which was okay temporarily, but, once he had made enough money to get his own place, then, he

could begin the actual preparation. After a few weeks, he could afford
to rent an efficiency apartment on the edge of town and then buy
a 'junker' at a used-car lot. He would need the apartment for only
a short time because he knew it would not take long for his plan to
be ready for action.

He collected everything he would need to create the mask:
liquid rubber, silicon, synthetic-based chemicals, nylon mesh, certain
colored dyes and various instruments. He even used a bowling ball
to serve as a skull on which to mold and shape the mask. His surgical
skills were kept in practice at the prison and he never lost his genius
touch to form a new face...like molding clay. This time, however,
his magical talent would not be used for any humanitarian purpose.

Now, the only thing left to do was obtain a picture of Wilbur,
but, he wasn't sure how to find one. After about two weeks of not
being able to come up with anything, he was starting to get worried
that this might be a bigger problem than he had anticipated. Then,
he saw a picture of me and Wilbur in the newspaper along with a
story about a local charity event we both attended. This, he thought,
might be just what he needed.

He cut out the picture of Wilbur and downloaded it onto a
computer at the library. Then, he enlarged and enhanced it, and,
super-imposed it on a grid where it could be duplicated three-
dimensionally. From that image, he would sculptor a mask that
looked exactly like Wilbur's face. And, coincidently, he was very
close to the height and build of Wilbur, which was crucial to the
success of the switch.

He was going to get to me by masquerading as my trusted aide.

Since he knew, from the local news, that the state police still had
an APB out on him, staying close-by was a good idea, he thought,
since they were probably assuming he would try to flee to Mexico
or South America. He had to become invisible and he figured that
not running would be the best way to elude capture by blending in
with the locals. My compound was located only 35 miles from the
town in which he was holed-up so he wasn't going to run anyway,
it was exactly where he wanted to be. But, if someone recognized
him, the game would be over, and, the thought of getting sent back
to the slammer for the remainder of his life with no possibility for
parole without completing his mission was not an option for him.

His scheme to exact his revenge on the man who obliterated his life, was almost ready to be implemented. He just needed to go to the courthouse one more time to absolutely confirm the timing of the activities. He had been to the courthouse numerous times before and had gotten to the point where he felt like he knew the routines like the back of his hand.

For example: One of the key ingredients of the plan was Wilbur's habit of using the restroom as soon as everyone was cleared out of the courtroom. He always hung back as long as he could while people were leaving and always saw Wilbur walk down the hall to the toilet, so, he had to rely on that happening again.

The final step would be, when the deed was done, fleeing the scene and disappearing. Go somewhere where he would never be apprehended...where he wouldn't have to be in disguise all the time and be careful of his every move. Somewhere where he could thumb his nose at the great American court system and proudly proclaim he won the final battle of his war against false justice run amok. He would be convinced, being the pathological ego-maniac that he was, that he was, indeed, the ultimate victor over a corrupt system of which he was such a tragic victim.

His plan for the last phase of his operation was rather simple: After beating my head to mush, he would go down to the dock and jump on my fishing boat. He read about and studied the ignition systems of certain boats on the internet in the prison library, so, he would be prepared if the keys were not in the ignition. And, since I lived on the gulf, he figured I would have some sort of a boat big enough for his purpose. Plus, he also knew that those boats carry a large reserve gas tank which should always be full, so, he wasn't worried about the motor sputtering out in the rough waters of the gulf's Southern rim.

After hot-wiring the engine, he would full-throttle out into the Gulf of Mexico, cruise South under the cover of darkness, about three miles out from shore, and head for Cuba.

THE FINALE

THE TIME FINALLY arrived when he knew he was ready. It was forecast to be cloudy, which would be an added assist for the success of his plan, so, today, it would all come down.

He had shaved his beard and got a haircut the day before so the mask would fit properly. His hair had to look as close to Wilbur's as possible, but, the fact that he was also going to wear a ball cap like Wilbur wore in the picture in the paper would allow that it wouldn't have to be a perfect look-alike.

Everything he had accumulated since he moved into his efficiency apartment would be left behind. There wasn't much...some clothes, a small TV, stale food in the fridge, empty beer bottles and all the paraphernalia from the mask-making process. He was even going to leave the gun he had taken from the dead guard at the accident as sort of a "nice try, but, you missed me" present for the authorities when they do eventually locate his hide-out/apartment and find the evidence. It won't matter what they find or when they find it, he thought, because by this time tomorrow he'll be drinking rum and smoking a big cigar in Havana while savoring the satisfaction of his long-awaited payback. How sweet it will be.

He had been to Cuba a couple of times before, at the request of Castro, (even he knew of Roth's reputation) to work in a Havana hospital to restore the faces of some of the soldiers of his private-guard who were attacked by rebel forces when they were on a special-ops patrol. The State Department sanctioned the two trips as a "goodwill gesture," and, he subsequently became a friend and 'confidant' of Fidel while he was there. Castro was very impressed by Roth's talent in the operating room and he treated him very well by providing lavish accommodations and anything else he wanted. Fidel told him one night over dinner with a big smile (in Spanish), "I hear so much about you before, but, now, I get to see you perform in person. You are good for my country...you are good for Fidel."

Remembering that resounding endorsement of their friendship, Roth figured all he had to do was show up at the front door of Fidel's palace and he would let him stay there for as long as he wanted. And, he knew the American authorities could not touch him.

One other detail that he had considered as a critical factor of his plan was that if he drove to the courthouse that day, the security guards would notice his car still parked in the lot after everyone else had left at the end of the day and that would definitely raise a red flag. Instead of locking up and going home like they usually do, they would go back to the garden, and, then, the courthouse, to look for the person who drove it there. That would be disaster.

Roth would not need a car that day because, this time, there would be no drive home. But, how would he get there?

His solution was to befriend a young Mexican named Pedro, with whom he worked at the auto shop. He was a nice guy...very friendly... always smiling. They struck up a good friendship, one that Roth had intentionally pushed along with a constant barrage of friendly chatter. He wanted to tie all the loose ends together so he could put the hammer down as soon as possible and Pedro would be the one that would provide the last critical factor of the equation.

They ate lunch together. They told jokes and laughed at each other. Roth was even talking to him about me over the last few weeks and was gradually working him over...telling him how great "this Judge Ed guy" is and that everybody should go see him in action at least once.

After a while, Pedro became very curious about me and told Roth he would like to visit my courthouse sometime, which was just what he wanted to hear. Roth told him he'd be glad to take him the next time he went, and, he would even buy a ticket for him for some weekday when they were both off from work. Pedro gave the big thumbs-up.

When Roth checked the work schedule for the next week, he saw that they both had Wednesday off. That day would be just right, so, he told Pedro that would be the day they would go.

The next day at work, Roth asked Pedro, very apologetically, if it would it be okay if he would drive to the courthouse next week because his car wasn't running right, and, since it was about a 35 mile drive each way, he didn't want to take the chance of getting stranded...out there where the alligators are walking around. He would even pay for the gas.

Pedro blurted, "Si–Si...I will do it for you."

Even though Roth was using Pedro as a pawn in his evil game, he found himself actually liking the guy. He really didn't want to get close to anybody, for obvious reasons, but, he liked Pedro because of his happy attitude toward life. He was sort of a respite for Roth...a diversion from his warped world of hate and revenge. Roth even felt a little guilty that he was taking advantage of Pedro, but, his prison-hatched mission to take me down was the only reason he was in this town and his cultivated friendship with Pedro meant very little when compared to that.

Granted, the police probably will track Pedro down after I'm long gone to Cuba, Roth thought, and put him on the grill to find out what he knew.

"Ok, Pedro, tell us what your involvement with Roth was all about and don't try to get cute, we know that you and Roth were good friends and always were talking at work. We have three witnesses from the auto shop who told us you and him were always hangin' together."

"No...honest, detective, I thought he was just a nice man...you know...my amigo. He was good to me...I didn't know he was a murderer. We just laughed together. He never said anything to me about murder"

But, in the end, there was no way they could charge him with aiding and abetting because the poor guy had no idea what the hell was going on and the cops couldn't prove otherwise.

It was time to go. Roth checked to make sure he had everything he needed, turned out the lights in his apartment and walked out to his car. As he got in and started the engine, a heinous grin slowly widened on his face that would have made The Grinch proud, and, then, he backed out of his parking spot and drove off for the last time.

He headed over to Pedro's apartment, as was pre-arranged, and parked his car in the street right in front. He left the keys in the ignition ("Someone else can drive it now...it worked okay for me"), got out and walked up to the door. He had only knocked twice when

Pedro yanked the door open and was standing there with a big smile on his face.

Roth said, "Are you ready to head down the road, amigo?"

Pedro shouted, "I am ready to go."

They both were laughing as they hopped in his pick-up. After Pedro slowly inched out on the street from the parking lot, he suddenly jammed his foot down on the accelerator and laid two streaks of rubber on the asphalt as he sped down the road...screaming out of the window "Arriba...Arriba." Roth tensed up a little and nervously shuffled his feet. He glanced over at Pedro with a uneasy grin and told him to take it easy and relax, that they were not in that big of a hurry. The last thing Roth needed was for Pedro to be pulled over by some traffic cop who just happened to be parked on the corner looking for trouble.

Roth's mind flashed with an imagined scene that gave him very bad vibes: After pulling us over, the cop slowly strolls up to Pedro's car, peers in the window at us both and tips his hat back a little and smiles. After the obligatory, "Good morning, sir," the cop would then ask to see Pedro's license and registration. Then, just out of curiosity, he would ask to see his ID, too. How would he respond?

"Why...uh...yes, officer...let's see...oh...I must have left it back at my place. I don't know how I could forget it... I'm terribly sorry, I always carry it with me. Ever since I fell and bumped my head on the stove last month, I seem to forget things more often. I'm supposed to see a doctor next Monday."

He didn't know if a pathetic line like that would work, but it didn't matter because they were now headed out of town, just passing the city limit sign, and, it was nothing but clear sailing.

As they were en route, Pedro commented to Roth about how much younger he looked without his beard and long hair. Roth said thanks. Then, he told Pedro how much he appreciated him driving, and, that he had arranged a ride home afterward with another friend he was meeting there, so, he could go ahead and leave without him and he would see him at work the next day.

As he sat in the last row with Pedro and watched the man he loathed admonish the defendants who stood, one by one, in front of the courtroom, he knew he was only going to get one chance. But, he was confident that one chance was all he was going to need. He wasn't nervous...too much time and planning had taken place for him to be hesitant or apprehensive now. His hands were steady and he was completely focused.

The last perp was finally led out of the courtroom and taken, with the rest of the defendants, to a Sheriff's van waiting in the parking lot to be hauled back to the jail in town. They were always escorted out before the spectators were allowed to leave. One time, one of the defendants got loose from a deputy who had him by the arm as they were walking up the walkway to the lot. He hollered out, "This is the last chance I got." He elbowed the deputy in the ribs and took off running back down toward the courthouse. The spectators were just then strolling out and the ones in front were suddenly startled to see this punk running crazy at them with two deputies chasing behind. No one knew what to do. Then, a man jumped out of the crowd and sprinted over and tackled him into some shrubs and completely subdued him in 5 seconds. When the deputies got there they thanked him for the help and the man said, "No problem...I enjoyed that...I'm an ex-Marine. I wish a couple more of 'em had gotten loose."

Roth stood up and started to file out to the lobby with the other visitors. He made sure he was at the back of the pack. He told Pedro he was going to hang back a little longer to meet his friend, so, he should go ahead and take-off. They shook hands and said goodbye. Pedro smiled and said, "See you tomorrow." Roth smiled back.

He waited for the exact time when he knew the guards would be distracted while they were holding the doors open and making sure everyone exited safely, and, then, doubled-back to the restroom area and waited for Wilbur in the corner. He knew that the video surveillance was turned off inside the courtroom and hallway after it was empty. He also knew that the three inside guards would eventually usher the people out the front door and through the garden toward the parking area. Very seldom did a guard come back to see if there were any stragglers in the lobby. This day, no one did.

Once the visitors were in their vehicles and driving back out to the road, the security crew, and, the two parking lot guards, would follow them out, lock the gate and go home. This routine was also crucial...getting a ride with Pedro meant he would not have to worry about any interference from them.

Wilbur finally showed up, but, a few minutes later than he normally did. Roth was starting to sweat it a little bit because he knew there was no time to spare...he had to stay on schedule. He needed to dispose of Wilbur, exchange clothes and put the mask on, and, then, get out of the front door before it was locked automatically by the security system.

Then, he would walk around the side of the courthouse through the bushes to the back. Here, if the timing of everything was right on, he would meet up with me just as I started down the pathway from the back door. So, Wilbur showing up at the restroom later than usual put an extra urgency to his time-line.

Wilbur never saw him lurking behind the potted plant, as he went in the restroom. Roth moved to just outside the door and stood there for a few moments making sure no one was coming back down the hallway, and, then, went in and locked the door behind him. He quickly came up from behind him as he was washing his hands at the sink and grabbed him around the neck. Then, he smothered his mouth and nose with a rag soaked with Ether that he had been keeping in a sealed plastic baggie in his pocket. Roth had no beef with Wilbur and had no intent of harming him, he just needed to get him out of the way for a while.

Wilbur struggled only a few seconds and then went limp. Roth laid him down in the corner and pulled off his pants and shirt. Then, he took off his own pants and shirt and put on Wilbur's clothes. He went over to the mirror and slid on the mask that he had hidden under his shirt ever since he left his apartment, and, made the adjustments so it contoured with his face perfectly. The first purpose of the mask was to give him some insurance that if he was seen by a guard or on camera, there would be no cause for alarm.

Then, he went out the door and headed down the hall to the lobby. He looked at his watch...he had 20 seconds to get out the door.

He made it through the door, and, as soon as he stepped down off the last step in front, he heard a loud click which meant the door was just locked.

He knew I always left the building by the rear door approximately 15 minutes after the last case because during each of his visits he hung around the garden with some other folks when they were walking to the parking lot and could see me walking down the path to the house through the trees and noticed the time on his watch. By using this timed schedule, he figured to attack me as I was walking down the path. He would have to use a large stick or rock that he would pick up off the ground as he was trailing me down to the house. He knew he couldn't get a gun or knife through the metal detector so these were the only weapons available, but, it didn't matter, they would do just fine...this was the way he wanted it anyway.

But, one thing that Roth could not have known was the fact that Wilbur's asthma inhaler, which he had just used ten minutes before being ambushed, coated the membranes of his trachea and lungs sufficiently to prevent the capillaries from absorbing most of the Ether and negated it's full effect.

He was out for only a few minutes, and, when he regained consciousness and his brain finally cleared, he knew something bad was going to happen. He immediately put on the pants and shirt that Roth had left and then ran out of the door to go warn me.

After I left the courthouse, I walked down the path, past the house and down to the tank to make sure the doors to the observation room were closed. Wilbur's tardiness to the restroom threw Roth's timing off a little because he wanted to bushwhack me on the path before I got to the house, but, he got to the path a couple minutes late and just missed me, so, he had to trail me further on down.

When I got up on the deck, I glanced back and thought I saw Wilbur walking down the path and then head over toward the tank where I was standing. The dogs, pacing in their pen because I had not gone over to let them out yet, were suddenly barking unusually loud, but, I thought they had seen a lizard or something, so, I didn't pay much attention.

Just as I was about to holler at him to check the door on the other side, I saw someone else running down the path and I had to do a double-take because he looked like Wilbur, too. Because of the heavy clouds, it was an unusually dark late afternoon so I had trouble seeing their faces clearly, which was what Roth had hoped.

Then, I heard Wilbur holler at me, "Watch out, Judge Ed."

My first reaction was to reach under my sweatshirt and pull out my Beretta handgun.

By then, Roth had walked up the ramp to the deck and was slowly walking around the edge of the tank toward me. When he heard Wilbur call out, he turned and saw him running down the path. This was something on which he had not planned...how could this happen?

He also had not counted on me packing heat.

The main purpose of the mask was that it would buy him enough extra time to get close to me and keep me from being alarmed until it was too late. He knew he couldn't speak to me because I would certainly know he wasn't Wilbur by the sound of his voice. He would just casually walk up to me, without saying a word, and cave in my skull before I could react and defend myself.

But, now, with the real Wilbur on the loose and coming to the rescue, he had to create a diversion to allow time for him to get around the deck and do the damage with the rock he was holding in his hand behind his back. So, he pointed over toward Wilbur and yelled, "Judge Ed...look out for that guy... he's a fake."

Then, he looked back at me and saw the gun.

By then, Wilbur had run up on the deck, and, before Roth could make his move, I told them both to freeze.

They were now both on the opposite side of the tank from me, about ten feet apart, staring down the barrel of my Beretta. From where I was standing, I really couldn't get a good look at their faces in the dim light...they were both too far away, but, I figured it wouldn't take long to identify the real Wilbur.

Then, Wilbur started yammering about what just happened in the restroom and how he knew he had to hurry down here to save my life. When he pointed at himself and shouted, "It's me, boss, I'm Wilbur...honest," that settled it...he was the real deal.

I yelled at Wilbur to walk around the rim of the tank toward me. Then, I ordered Roth to lie down on his stomach with his hands behind his head. I wanted to give Wilbur my cell phone to call the police and also have him punch in the code to lower the spikes in the road so they could get to the house.

Then, it hit me...I suddenly realized who this guy was...he had to be Roth.

When he first escaped, the police told me he was on the loose and said to be cautious until they found him, but, they thought he was out of the area so there wasn't really anything to worry about. After a few weeks, I sort of let my guard down thinking he must be long-gone because if he was going to try something, he would have done it by now. But, here he was, standing directly across from me wearing a mask...like it was Halloween.

As I glanced over at Wilbur and began to tell him what I wanted him to do, Roth thought I was distracted enough that he could make a last dash for me. But, before he went five feet, I shot him in the right leg and he went down hard on the deck, right by the edge of the tank. Blood was streaming down his leg from the bullet hole and dripping into the water.

The pain of the bullet, and, the realization that his carefully planned seven-year mission of revenge had been sabotaged by the same man who destroyed his life intensified his rage. He rolled back and forth on the wooden planks, holding his leg, wailing and hollering things at me I couldn't understand.

He then started to squirm on his belly while blood was still oozing out of his leg, and, using his hands to pull him over the slats, he clawed at the deck looking for the rock he dropped when I shot him.

He kept moaning, "The rock...I gotta find that rock...where the hell is my rock?" It was a pathetic sight. Obviously, he had not seen the rock roll into the tank when he let go of it when he first went down.

Then, he stopped, became quiet and lay motionless. He wasn't dead because I could see his chest heave as he was sucking for air.

As I was debating what to do next, suddenly, he totally freaked-out and jumped up and started to run at me again. I couldn't believe it. But, he didn't get far. He lost his balance after about two steps and fell in the water before I could shoot him in the other leg. He began thrashing around as he was desperately trying to get to the side and pull himself back up on the deck.

And, then, he turned and saw the fins slicing through the water toward him. In an instant, he realized his horrific fate. He looked up at me and screamed, "I'll see you in Hell."

That I understood loud and clear.

Once he had gone in, I knew there was no way to get him out in time. The only thing that Wilbur and I could do now was watch. The sharks had been on high alert ever since they smelled the blood that dripped into the water from the bullet wound. Once they heard the splash of Roth's body, they went into a total frenzy and wasted no time as they darted over, converged on him from both sides and immediately ripped off both of his arms.

He screamed again...for the last time.

Then, the Tiger shark chomped down on his chest and shook him like a rag doll. And, as Roth stared back at me through the cut-out holes in the mask with his eyes filled with utter terror, the shark pulled him under and took him to the bottom. Wilbur and I stood in silence and watched as the water churned and bubbled. And, then, began to turn red as billows of blood started to permeate to the surface.

After a few minutes, the water became calm again. The sharks had finished their meal and resumed their perpetual slow glide around the circumference of the tank as if nothing had happened.

Wilbur and I had seen enough. The adrenalin in my veins had stopped it's surge, and, the physical and mental intensity that had consumed my body for the last ten minutes was now waning, and, my mood was changing to a sense of relief and disgust.

I told Wilbur, "let's get out of here."

He said, "Yeah, let's go, I've had enough fun for one day."

As we started to walk over to the ramp and head back up to the house to call the police, I looked back at the tank one more time, and, just then, a shoe popped to the surface...and, then, the mask.

It was a fitting end for the man who dared to tangle with...The Honorable Judge Ed.

The End